Tormented by guilt for the danger that Elice and her family are in, Cabot makes a painful decision.

"I won't be back," he said quietly, staring at the floor.

Elice didn't say a word. She seemed to be waiting for him to take back what he'd said. When he didn't speak, she slumped into a dining room chair and said, "I never blamed you for anything that happened."

She sat there, hands folded primly in her lap, her jaw set, her shoulders back. It was her "hold the tears back" stance, he knew, and he felt even worse knowing he'd pushed her this far. He held his head in his hands and prayed for the strength to do what must be done.

"I love you," she said softly. "You can't hide from that. No matter how far away you go."

Cabot sprung to his feet and stomped around the dining room. "I'm not hiding, Elice. I'm. . .I'm trying to guarantee your safety."

She stood, too, and carried a pile of dirty dishes to the kitchen sink. "By leaving me? You're ridiculous." Elice put the stack of plates onto the kitchen counter with a clatter.

"Maybe so," he admitted, "but I'm also dangerous."

LOREE LOUGH lives in Ellicott City, Maryland. She is a wife and the mother of two daughters. Loree makes her *Heartsong Presents* debut with *Pocketful of Love*.

Pocketful of
Love

Loree Lough

Heartsong Presents

To my family, who fills all the pockets of my heart with love. TMM:YKW

ISBN 1-55748-559-3

POCKETFUL OF LOVE

one

Thick, dark hair swirled around her shoulders as she turned toward the sound of his closing car door.

"Who do I see about having a sign painted?" he asked.

She dropped the weed she'd just picked onto the pile with the others then stood and brushed the dirt from the knees of her jeans. "That'd be me."

He pocketed both hands and focused on the small child who ran toward them, a Popsicle clown-grin on her tiny face. "Mommy," she giggled, "it's leaking."

"What's leaking, Annie?"

"The place where the water comes out." Her pudgy hands flapped, imitating the flow of water.

Annie's mom closed her eyes and tilted her face toward the late afternoon sun, then took a deep breath. When she looked at him again, her face brimmed with amusement. "You'll have to excuse me, but I'd better see about this before we flood the valley."

He followed Annie and her mom into the backyard. Bright splashes of color shocked his senses. To him, planting involved only the seeds that became food. He was totally unfamiliar with those that produced such beauty. Subconsciously, he compared it to his own stark yard.

"See?" Annie squeaked, pointing to the spray of water coming from the hose. "It looks like a fountain, doesn't it, Mommy?"

He guessed the child's age at four or five. Lindy would have been seven. The big ache in his heart throbbed as he watched Annie break off the end of her Popsicle and watch the crimson line that crept toward her elbow. The last time he'd seen Lindy, he'd snapped a picture of her spaghetti-sauced grin. For an instant, he wondered where he'd put that photograph.

Annie's mom turned off the water, adjusted the hose more tightly to the spigot, then twisted the squeaking handle until the end of the hose spurted water once again. "You're right, sweetie. It did look like a fountain. Maybe you ought to stand under it and rinse off that sticky Popsicle juice."

When she faced him again, her brown eyes seemed to smile as brightly as her lovely mouth. "Sometimes I feel like Captain Kangaroo. . .without benefit of pocket entertainment," she said. "It's a madhouse around here, isn't it?"

Standing this close to the petite woman made him feel like a linebacker. "Not at all," he said, assessing the freshly mowed lawn and the tidy flower beds. "Things seem very organized. Your husband must have ten green thumbs. I don't think I've so many flowers—"

"My mommy calls them little presents from God," Annie injected, chewing the tip of one blond braid. "But she doesn't have a husband. First he runned away. Then he died."

He tried not to stare at the agonized, embarrassed expression, partially hidden behind the mother's hands.

She took a deep breath and said, her voice trembling slightly, "Annie, go inside and ask Emi to stir the soup."

Annie glanced toward the screen door. "But, Mommy. . . she's right there. You could tell her yourself."

The gentle smile vanished. Her left brow rose high on her forehead as she tucked in one corner of her mouth. Then, aiming her pointer finger at the child, she said, "I'd like you to tell her. And ask her to call the Becks and have them send Danny home. It's nearly supper time."

Annie stuck the dry braid into her mouth, wide blue eyes deciphering her mother's demeanor. Without a word, she looked at her bare toes, then turned and disappeared into the house.

"Twin Acres Signs comes very highly recommended," he said, closing the subject of her missing-then-dead husband. "I saw the one you painted for the Becks. Good work." He wondered how her husband could have left a woman with such a sweet, innocent face.

But her past really didn't matter one bit to him. He'd decided long ago that living life alone was far easier than loving—and losing. Her business was painting signs. He wanted one. Period. "Cabot Murray," he said, extending a hand.

She grasped it firmly and without a moment's hesitation. "Elice Glasser." She nodded toward the garage. "That's my workshop." She headed for the double-doored building. "Follow me," Elice said, "and we'll see about that sign of yours."

Inside, Cabot surveyed the clutter-free workbench. Inventoried power tools. Saw tape measures and wood files that hung in order by size on the pegboard behind the slanted draftsman's table. On the opposite wall, jars of paint thinner and cans of varnish stood in orderly rows on metal shelves. On a big drafting table across the room, lay a sign in-progress. Clean paintbrushes of all shapes and sizes poked out of a tall tin can. Here, as in the yard, perfection.

"Can you really use all this equipment?"

She dropped onto the squeaking seat of an ancient secretarial chair. "Yup."

His heart did a little flip when she punctuated her answer with a merry wink. The reaction surprised him, since he'd always been partial to tall, blue-eyed blonds.

Still, something nagged inside him. Except for the husband story, things seemed entirely too perfect in Elice Glasser's world. And, if his former cop-life had taught him anything, it was that perfection didn't exist. He wondered what Elice Glasser was hiding behind that perfect façade.

"What kind of sign did you have in mind?" Her hair hid her face as she rummaged in a desk drawer. It seemed to annoy her. She grabbed a rubber band from the table top and pulled her thick hair into a loose ponytail.

Cabot shrugged, strangely disappointed that she'd imprisoned all those gorgeous curls. "Something that says Foggy Bottom Farm."

She looked up and met his eyes, then smiled. "What a nice, peaceful name."

His heart did the little flip again. Without all that hair around it, her face seemed more noticeable. He'd heard of heart-shaped faces and guessed they'd be pointy-bottomed, horrid little things. He'd been dead wrong. Cabot pocketed both hands. "My dad named the place. I'm just carrying on tradition."

"You take a look at that," she said, handing him the booklet she'd pulled from the drawer, "while I whip up a sample sketch." Using her foot, she slid an old metal stool closer to her drafting table. "Make yourself at home."

As he took the booklet, he couldn't help but notice her rough, reddened hands and closely cut fingernails. He hung the heels of his scuffed work boots on the stool's bottom rung and pretended to study lettering styles. But Cabot never really saw the pages; he was too busy remembering the pained expression that darkened her bright eyes when Annie blurted out all that stuff about her daddy. Elice obviously still felt the pain of his leaving quite intensely; the look on her face had been proof enough of that. Cabot wondered what kind of man would leave a gorgeous wife and three kids.

"How's that?" she asked.

He'd been staring, and she'd caught him at it. Cabot coughed to hide his blush and took the sketch from her work-hardened hand. In just over a minute, she'd centered the words "Foggy Bottom Farm" in a bold arch, the western lettering so precise it reminded him of the sign above the blacksmith's shop in Williamsburg, Virginia. Elice's husband and why he left grew less and less important as Cabot added "talented" to his growing list of her attributes.

"I guess you'll want the standard size—two feet by three—same design on both sides?"

Cabot nodded.

Elice nodded, too, as if she'd expected him to agree. "Just a plain rectangle, or some fancy curves?"

"Plain and simple, that's my style." Plain and simple is your style? he repeated mentally. Where'd that come from!

"I'll put your family name here," she said, reaching across his chest to point at the space she'd left beneath "Foggy Bottom."

Cabot forced himself to stare at the drawing. Being a cop all those years had honed his ability to see many things at once. His eyes were on the drawing, but it was Elice he saw. Her dark hair made him think of his grandmother's old mink stole, gleaming with red and gold highlights. He inhaled the clean, fresh scent of her shampoo and wondered if the curls would feel as soft as they looked.

He cleared his throat. "How soon will it be ready?"

She lifted the calendar page and squinted at the bold, black numerals. Clicking the pencil's eraser against her bottom teeth, she said, "Two weeks, give or take a day."

But she was a widow. With three kids to raise, a house and two-acre spread to tend, and a business to run. "There's no rush. I'm back in Freeland for good."

He watched as her brows knitted, as if she didn't understand what his being back in town had to do with how long it would take to complete the sign. But then, he wasn't surprised. Everything about her was a contradiction: soft hair, rough hands; velvety eyes, hard life; sweet voice, tough businesswoman. The contrasts caused a bubbling warmth deep in his stomach, and Cabot didn't know what to make of it. *Nothing ventured, nothing lost*, he reminded himself. "Just call me when it's finished," he said, sounding more abrupt and harsh than he'd intended.

She leaned back in her chair. The clock on the wall said tick-tock, tick-tock. In that instant, he recognized the look on her face as one he'd seen hundreds of times as he had interrogated witnesses. It told him she was trying to figure out whether or not his tone had been one of anger.

"Standard price is a hundred dollars." Her voice sounded as smooth and sweet as honey, despite her businesslike words. "Half down, to get me started, the other half when I'm finished."

They faced each other for a long, silent moment, like old West gunfighters, waiting to see who'd draw first. He reminded himself he'd come here to order a sign. He hadn't had a decent night's sleep or a real meal in days and had avoided any semblance of family for years. The romantic stuff tumbling around in his head he chalked up to deprivation. But he knew he'd better get away from this place, fast, or his life's motto would be a distant memory.

"Sounds like a fair price to me," he said.

The guys on the force had nicknamed him Speedy Gonzales because he'd always moved with lightning speed.

When he reached for his billfold, Elice flinched. Cabot froze. He'd seen that reaction, too, in his street cop days. It told him she'd been abused. He wanted to tell her he wouldn't dream of hurting her. At the same time, he wanted to throttle the man who'd put such fear into those beautiful brown eyes. The clock tick-tocked some more while he tried to think of something clever, something soothing to say. His big hands trembled as he thumbed through the bills in his wallet. "I. . .uh. . .I seem to be a little short. . . ."

"You're not short," Annie said. "You're tall. Very tall."

He'd been so involved in Elice's fright that Cabot hadn't even noticed the little girl enter the workshop. As she stood there, looking up at him with those big blue eyes of hers, he wanted to scoop her up, give her a huge hug, and kiss that Popsicle-red smile of hers. He met Elice's eyes. She'd composed herself quickly, he acknowledged. If he hadn't seen it himself, he'd never have guessed that only moments ago, she had looked for all the world like a terrified child. "It won't take but a minute to run home and get my checkbook. My cupboards are as bare as Old Mother Hubbard's," he said, chuckling, "and I have to do some grocery shopping anyway; I'll be passing right by—"

"'Old Mother Hubbard went to the cupboard to get her poor dog a bone,'" Annie said, grinning, as she recited the Mother Goose nursery rhyme. "Do you have a dog?"

Cabot laughed. "No. I don't."

Annie shook her head and frowned. "Me, either. Mommy says she doesn't have time for a fuzzy kid with four legs." She headed for the door, stretching the pink straps of her bathing suit. "Emi says to tell you the table is set and Danny's on his way home." She gave Cabot a quick once-over, then looked back at her mother. "Is he eating supper with us, Mommy?"

She glanced from her daughter to Cabot and back again. "He just stopped by to order a sign, sweetie," Elice said. "I'm sure he has better things to do than eat day-old bread and soup."

Maggie had called Lindy "honey" in exactly that same motherly tone of voice. The dull ache in Cabot's heart grew as Annie planted herself directly in front of him and asked, "Do you have any kids?"

Cabot shook his head, then squatted to make himself child-sized. "I had a little girl once, but she died." It surprised him how easily the words came tumbling out. What surprised him more was that saying them didn't hurt this time.

"Couldn't you and your wife get another one?"

He swallowed hard. "I'm afraid she's dead, too."

She placed a tiny hand on his cheek. "That's too bad," she said, blinking her huge blue eyes, the blond brows above them rising in sympathy.

Cabot didn't dare look at Elice. If he saw even a trace of pity on her face, he'd flee the workshop like a man being chased by a nightmare. Because that's exactly what he was, and he knew it.

Her hand clamped on her daughter's shoulder, the sweet, maternal tone replaced by one of no nonsense: "Annie, go inside and wash up for—"

Annie's brows rose high on her forehead as she folded her tiny hands in front of her chest. "Oh, Mommy," she said, turning to hug Elice's knees, "he's all alone. Can't the nice man stay for supper? Please?"

Cabot resisted the urge to bolt from the workshop, fire up his Jeep, and head back to Foggy Bottom as fast as he could. Then he realized he was still holding his wallet. Standing, he closed it and cleared his throat. "I'll. . .uh. . .I'll stop by later with the money," he stammered, stuffing it into his back pocket.

Annie's bare feet made tiny slapping sounds on the concrete floor as she followed him to the door. "What's your name?" she asked, grabbing his big hand.

He stared at the tiny hand in his. "Cabot. Cabot Murray."

Frowning, Annie looked at the big hand that surrounded hers. "How'd you get so dirty, Mr. Murray?"

"Annie, if I have to tell you one more time to go inside . . .," Elice warned.

Smiling, he met Elice's eyes at last. "It's okay. I don't mind." He faced Annie. "This stuff is called axle grease. You see, I've been working on my tractor all day."

Annie shook her head and frowned. "Mommy doesn't like dirty hands. 'Specially at the table." She glanced at Elice, then whispered, "Grandma gave me some neat soap for my birthday. It will make you smell like flowers. Maybe once you're clean, Mommy will let you stay for supper."

"Annie. . . ." Elice's voice was a mixture of warning and amusement. "I'm going to count to three, and if you're not inside washing those hands by the time—"

Immediately, the child released Cabot's hand and headed for the door. "Okay, okay, I'm going."

When she was out of earshot, Elice frowned. "Sorry about that. I don't know what gets into her sometimes."

"There's absolutely nothing to apologize for. I think she's adorable." *And so are you*, he thought. Twin Acres had a strange and mystical hold on him. He knew if he didn't get out of there, and quick, he'd lose all control over his emotions. He needed time to get things straight in his head. Lots of time.

"I'll stop by in the morning with the deposit," he promised. And then he left, without a word, without so much as a backward glance. Cabot had faced armed gunmen in dark alleys, stood eye to eye with drug dealers, thieves, robbers, killers. But none had caused such a mixture of confusion and fear in him because while he could easily explain his feelings toward the bad guys, he sensed that one more moment in her company, and he may as well kiss his life's motto goodbye. Doing that scared him more than any of those bad guys.

When Maggie and Lindy died, he rewrote the old cliché to fit his new, solitary lifestyle and "Nothing ventured, nothing gained" became "Nothing ventured, nothing lost." He threw himself so completely into his work that the loneliness didn't attack—until darkness closed in. Sometimes a good mystery novel or a spirited baseball game on TV knocked it out. But now, for the first time since their deaths, loneliness attacked in the daytime, too. And it was harder, more painful to look at in the bold light of day.

When his farmhouse finally came into view through the windshield, emptiness echoed loudly within him. "Find something to take your mind off it," he told himself, parking the Jeep, then slamming its door. "Just get busy and you'll—"

Cabot noticed it the moment he started up the back walk. He'd locked that door. He was certain of it. A familiar tension knotted in his gut as he hurried inside and peered around. The kitchen looked exactly as he'd left it, right down to the half-filled coffee cup and slice of cold toast he'd left on the table.

Except for the blue slip of paper that leaned against the salt and pepper shakers in the middle of the table. On it was the message: *Go back where you came from, cop, before innocent people get hurt.*

❧

No matter how busy she kept herself, Elice couldn't get

Cabot Murray out of her mind.

She'd been a widow for nearly three years and had been without a husband two long years before that. In those first lonely days, her solitary status frightened her. But soon, as she began taking on more and more responsibility—and succeeding—she began to like being on her own, being in charge of her own destiny. She learned that the more she concentrated on the many things about her life for which she could be thankful, the happier she felt. Her dad willed her the house and two acres upon which it sat. Her kids were physically fit, well behaved, and well adjusted; Twin Acres Signs was a thriving business. She'd accomplished a lot, all on her own, but Elice never let a day begin or end without thanking God for her many blessings.

It hadn't always been that way, of course. When Bobby first left, she couldn't understand how God could have let a man leave his pregnant wife and two small kids to fulfill a silly dream of driving race cars. She'd been hanging on by a thread, praying that God would guide Bobby home, when the call came informing her that Bobby's souped-up car had exploded, killing him instantly. When he died, a little bit of her innocence died with him. But, with that death came maturity and wisdom—something else for which to be thankful.

Yes, she liked her solitary lifestyle just fine. Elice came and went as she pleased, answering to no one but the Lord. She worked hard, and it showed. What had started as a hobby grew into a bustling business that sent the bill collectors packing and kept the kids well fed and clothed. Her first sign painting jobs were simple entrance signs for friends' and neighbors' farms. Gradually, her reputation had grown, until the little company she'd started from scratch on her dining room table was being commissioned by business and industry in northern Maryland and southern Pennsylvania.

Several eligible men had tried, unsuccessfully, to woo her, saying she was far too young and pretty to stay footloose and fancyfree for long. But Elice had no intention of marrying again. She'd made a huge error in judgment when she'd put all her faith and belief in Bobby Glasser. It had been at his graveside that she'd promised herself she'd never again put her children or herself through the kind of torture that goes hand-in-hand with the cold, self-centeredness of a non-believer.

And then Cabot Murray waltzed into her life, tall and blond and bronzed, with those glowing, knowing, hazel eyes.

She'd never liked the strong, silent type, but something about him appealed to her. Elice suspected he hid a softer, gentler side beneath that rough-and-tough exterior. She'd seen a glimmer of it in his golden eyes when he had squatted to talk with Annie in the workshop.

Marge King, who knew everything about everybody in Freeland, had told Elice that Cabot had earned a full academic scholarship to attend the University of Illinois. He'd been the school's starting quarterback for three years running. After graduation, he had become a uniformed Chicago street cop. He'd only been on the force two weeks when he sent for his fiancée, Maggie, and they were married in the Windy City. Five years later, he made detective. And he'd just celebrated his fifth year at that rank when his wife and daughter were killed in a car accident on the Dan Ryan Expressway.

Elice told herself God had allowed her to experience such full-hearted warmth toward the big stranger because Cabot had been away from his home town for such a long time and hadn't had a chance to rekindle old relationships. The

Lord wanted her, she believed, to extend a hand of friendship to the sad-eyed, lonely man.

Cabot had left Freeland when Elice was still in junior high school and though they'd shopped in the same stores, attended the same schools, even gone to the same church, their paths had never crossed. Now that they had, Elice felt obligated, being the first person he'd made real contact with in town, to be a good Christian in every sense of the word, and help him make the adjustment from the hustle and bustle of the big city to the slow-paced life of a farm community.

She decided that when he stopped by in the morning with the sign's deposit, she'd invite him to lunch or supper or maybe Sunday dinner. She giggled to herself as she thought, maybe all three; it's what any decent Christian would do, after all.

Elice pictured his broad shoulders and barrel chest. . .his narrow waist. . .the thick blond curls atop his handsome head. . .those piercing, dark-lashed, golden eyes, and the wide smile he seemed cautiously determined to keep all to himself. Her stomach fluttered and her heart pounded as she remembered the power of his handshake and the warmth of his big, calloused palm. Though she'd turned thirty-two on her last birthday, Elice had never experienced such a physical reaction to a man in her life. The feelings scared yet intrigued her, and she realized it would take all the strength she could muster to maintain her steady, independent lifestyle. "Lord," she said aloud, grinning, "I have a feeling I'm gonna be callin' on You a lot in the days to come."

❧

He'd run into Marge King at Nardi's grocery store, and now that Cabot had been told Elice Glasser's history, he knew why he'd been so attracted to the petite brunette. He'd always admired people who turned negatives into positives. And he'd never met an individual who'd turned a bigger minus into a plus better than Elice Glasser had.

According to Marge, everybody loved Elice and her kids. She'd become a legend of sorts, having survived what only a few others could have.

As the days passed, Cabot chopped enough wood to last six winters; he also thought of her. As he plowed the garden, he pictured her. While he mended fences, he heard her musical voice in his memory. No matter what task he undertook or how hard he worked at it, Cabot couldn't get her out of his head.

The top of her curly head barely reached his shoulder. From the looks of her, she couldn't weigh more than a hundred pounds, yet he'd seen her lift Annie, a hefty child of five or six, he guessed, as if she'd been light as a feather. Elice had grit. She was a marvelous blend of tender and tough, and he liked that. . .liked it a lot.

She moved like a fashion model, destroying the stereotype that only tall, willowy women carried themselves with grace and dignity. He liked that, too. When she smiled at Annie, her whole face got involved, from those dancing brown eyes to that adorable, dimpled grin. He'd never seen longer eyelashes on a human being. . .or creamier skin. And those freckles, sprinkled across the bridge of her nose, gave a little-girl quality to her womanly features. He liked that best of all.

Cabot dragged his shirtsleeve across his perspiring brow and leaned on the gate he'd just repaired. A movement in the pines at the north end of Foggy Bottom caught his attention. He'd seen a similar movement earlier and had dismissed it as a deer. Now, curiosity propelled him forward and he ran toward it full throttle, big booted feet thudding across the grassy meadow, eyes riveted to the spot where he'd last seen it. When Cabot reached the row of evergreens, he found nothing but confusion and fear, for no animal had caused the branches to move in that lazy, bouncing way, nor redistributed the fallen pine needles, nor cast that eerie, ghostlike shadow.

The chill had been gnawing at him like a hungry rat for weeks, ever since Clancy's call. "Deitrich is out," his former partner had said. "They released him more than a week ago. Just thought you oughta know."

Cabot had shrugged off the warning. Surely Deitrich wouldn't carry out the threat he'd made that day in the courtroom: "I won't rest till I see you dead, cop," he'd seethed as the guards dragged him, handcuffed and kicking, toward the paddy wagon that would deliver him to Joliet Prison. Chuckling, Cabot wished he had a dollar for every bad guy who'd threatened him that way. Once they got out of jail, convicts were usually too busy reconnecting with friends and loved ones, trying to make a go of the straight life to be bothered with making good on stupid threats.

Still, Deitrich had been different from most. His eyes bore no trace of human compassion; his smile never quite reached those steely gray orbs. And when he'd promised to see Cabot dead, his words hung in the muggy air for what seemed like a full minute before being swallowed up by the footsteps, paper shuffling, and muffled whispers.

Cabot had used the last of his energy speeding toward the shadow. Thirsty, he headed slowly back to the farmhouse. Then, standing at the kitchen sink, he gulped three glasses of cold water, one right after the other. Deitrich's threat was gonging in his head when the phone rang. It startled him so badly that he splashed the contents of a fourth glass down the front of his plaid work shirt.

"I hope I'm not interrupting your. . . ."

It had been nearly two weeks since he'd heard that musical voice, yet he recognized it immediately. Suddenly, Deitrich, the note, and the shadow in the pines were forgotten. "Not at all," he said, unaware of the width of his smile. "In fact, I just quit for the day."

"I wanted to let you know your sign is finished," Elice said.

"Already?" He tugged the front of his shirt to keep the cold, wet material away from his skin. Cabot checked his watch. If he didn't fool around, he could be showered and changed in half an hour. "I can pick it up this evening, if that's convenient."

He wished he could retract what he'd just said. Toss some warmth into his voice. Replace the formal vocabulary with friendlier, chattier talk. Cabot heard Annie's voice in the background: "Can he have supper with us tonight? Please, Mommy?"

Her voice was muffled and Cabot could almost see Elice standing there, one hand over the mouthpiece, the other holding the phone to her ear. "What is it with you and that Mr. Murray?" he heard her say.

"I like him," was the child's response. "He wants us to be his friends. I can tell."

When everything got loud again, he knew she'd uncovered the phone. She sighed deeply, then said, "If you're not busy, maybe you'd like to join us for supper tonight."

Nothing ventured, nothing lost, he thought. He considered telling her he already had plans. That he had a pot of stew on the stove. "What's on the menu?"

"Stuffed, roasted chicken. Mashed potatoes and gravy. Green beans," she recited, her voice a monotone. "Nothing fancy."

"I'll bring dessert. What time should I—"

"Six o'clock. And you don't need to bring anything. I just took an apple pie out of the oven."

He couldn't remember what she said after that, or what he'd said in response. Cabot could only concentrate on the fact that he was going to see her again.

The minute she said goodbye, he showered and shaved. He stood in his closet for fifteen minutes, trying to decide what to wear. He decided casual would send the best message, and chose blue jeans and a starched white shirt. But he'd polish his cowboy boots.

As he paced from the living room to the kitchen, Cabot glanced at his watch. Its hands seemed stuck at four-thirty. He considered taking it off, thinking maybe time would pass more quickly if he couldn't see the second hand flick slowly, slowly around the dial.

He sat at his desk and shuffled papers and refused to look at his watch. Cabot balanced his checkbook, paid a few bills, started a letter to Clancy and his dear wife then wadded it up and tossed it in the trash when he noticed he'd doodled "Elice" in the margin. When the mantle clock signaled five-thirty, his heart pounded.

She'd told him not to bring anything, but he wanted to stop at Nardi's and buy a bouquet of flowers, at least. Elice seemed to love them. Why else would she have surrounded the house with colorful blooms of every variety?

As he drove toward the neighborhood grocery store, "Nothing ventured, nothing lost" echoed in his mind. He drove straight past Nardi's. The smart thing to do, he told himself, is give the pretty lady her money, grab your sign, and tell them you forgot a previous engagement. And then get on out of there. . .nice and neat. . .and safe.

But he'd forgotten what a fool he'd always been for big,

sad eyes. His weakness seemed to have grown stronger as he aged for as he stood in the middle of the Glassers' sunny kitchen and made his rehearsed announcement, Annie's lower lip jutted out. Elice's bright eyes dimmed with disappointment. He felt like a heel. So he agreed to stay. But just this once, he promised himself. As soon as you clean up your plate, you'll hit the road. Hate to eat and run, he'd say, smiling politely, but I have a million things to do. . . .

Why did they have to be such nice kids? And why did their mom have to be so pretty? She was a good cook, too; he couldn't remember when homemade apple pie had tasted as good. Cabot found himself clearing the table, then standing beside her, towel drying each dish she washed. It was as if someone had buried a giant magnet under the tidy little house and he had a huge core of ore in the middle of him, because he couldn't seem to pry himself from the place.

When the dishes were done, she handed him a glass of iced tea and invited him to join her on the covered back porch.

"How old are they?" he asked, nodding toward her children, playing in the yard.

"Emily is ten. Danny's nine. And Annie's five."

He'd guessed eleven, eight, and six. Satisfied that his guess had been fairly accurate, he grinned. "It's hard to believe you're their mom. You don't look old enough to have kids at all."

"That's the oldest trick in the book," she teased.

Both blond brows rose in sincere confusion. "Trick?"

"I'm thirty-two, to answer your unasked question. Until next week, that is."

He grinned. "I don't believe it."

The phone rang and she dashed inside to answer it. He focused on Annie, digging happily in the sandbox, and Emily and Danny, who dangled from the tire swing that hung from a giant oak. When she returned, he saw a worry frown on her face. Impulsively, Cabot took her hand. "Hey, what's the matter?" he said, concern edging his voice as she sat in the lawn chair beside him. "Looks like you've seen a ghost."

She took a deep breath and squared her shoulders. "Oh, it was nothing. Just another one of those prank calls. It's been going on for a week or so. I wish parents would teach their kids that a telephone is not a toy."

Elice fidgeted, staring at their entwined hands. He let her go and leaned his elbows on his knees. "What does the caller say?"

"Nothing." The brave smile dimmed slightly. "I feel like I know the person, though. Isn't that strange?"

It wasn't the least bit strange. Plenty of ordinary folks had what cops referred to as "gut instinct," and he told her so.

"I wonder," she said, more to herself than to Cabot, "if the phone calls have anything to do with the doorbell—"

"Doorbell?"

She met his eyes briefly. But in that instant, he read her fear.

"Night before last, it rang in the middle of the night. When I looked outside, no one was there. That was the second time in two weeks—"

He was all cop now, his brows drawn together in concentration. "How many calls, altogether?"

"Ten. Fifteen, maybe." She shrugged helplessly.

"And two doorbell incidents in as many weeks?"

She nodded.

"When did all this weird stuff start?"

Her eyes locked with his as a grin formed on her lips. "You have too much hair to be Kojak, but you sure do sound like him."

Cabot blinked, stunned by her comment. Her smile was contagious. "Old habits die hard, I guess," he said. "Sorry. I was a cop—"

"In Chicago. I know," she finished.

He could tell by her tone that Freeland had been buzzing and that he'd been the main subject in the hive. He liked the way she looked when she smiled, and wanted to encourage more of it. "So tell me. . .how do you manage? It can't be easy, running a business, taking care of the house, raising three kids all by yourself. . . ."

She took a deep breath. "It was tough for a while there, but the Lord has been very good to us."

He wished he could accept what happened to Maggie and Lindy as well as Elice seemed to accept her lot in life. The accident had rendered him helpless. When the helplessness passed, bitterness set in. He'd been a devout Christian all his life, and his faith only got bigger with Maggie at his side. But without her. . . . How could he believe in a Being Who would allow two generous, loving people to die need-less, horrid deaths? Every day, Cabot saw the innocent vic-tims of violent crime. Where was God when all that may-hem was going on? he wanted to know. He must have de-manded an answer to that question a hundred times. But his question always went unanswered.

When he couldn't take any more death and suffering, he quit. Not just the police force, but God, too. Then he headed back to his birthplace, where life promised to be peaceful. And now Elice was being harassed by prank calls and a doorbell nut. Tranquil Freeland was beginning to sound an awful lot like Chicago, New York, L.A. And what are You gonna do about it, God? he wanted to know.

"Can I freshen your iced tea?" she asked, interrupting his

reverie. "It's decaffeinated."

Cabot glanced at his empty glass. The sun had set and dusk surrounded them. It would be dark soon. He knew he should leave so she could tuck her kids in and get some much needed rest. But he couldn't break away from that powerful magnetic force that was distinctly Twin Acres. Maybe if he hung around, whoever was pestering her would get scared and cut it out. He wasn't exactly a midget, after all. He grinned, admitting the real reason he didn't want to leave was standing beside him, hand extended to accept his empty glass. "I'd love more iced tea."

Once she'd refilled his glass, Elice led him into the living room and turned on the ball game. "The Orioles are playing Toronto tonight," she said. "I've been looking forward to this all day." Elice grinned and handed him the TV's remote, then turned her attention to the kids' bedtime ritual.

Elice had it all, all right. She was a terrific mom, a talented artist, a successful businesswoman. In addition she was pretty, sweet, a great cook, and a baseball fan, too! He didn't think a more perfect woman existed. From where he sat in the overstuffed forest green chair, he could see all the way to the other end of the house. His eyes rested for a moment on the stove, its chromed parts shining in the dim light. She had waxed the floor recently—had missed a spot. *So,* he thought, smiling, *she's not perfect after all.*

Listening to the giggling and babbling of her kids, Cabot recalled what Marge had said about Elice: "No matter what anybody else said, she insisted something good and decent lived in Bobby Glasser."

Helen, the cashier at Nardi's, had been listening: "She'd give you the shirt off her back, even if it meant she'd have to go without."

The women shook their heads. "She deserved better than

that low-life," Marge added.

"She'd trust a rattlesnake," the older woman put in. "I used to think she was addle-brained, she was so sweet."

Marge concluded: "They don't make 'em like Elice anymore."

They sure don't, Cabot thought, closing his eyes. Being in her house, surrounded by the laughter of children and the warm family atmosphere had forced him to reexamine his solitary lifestyle. At that moment, he didn't miss Lindy and Maggie in the same old hurting way. Rather, being at Twin Acres made him yearn for that companionable feeling that only a home filled with loved ones can bring.

"Resting your eyes?" Elice asked. She was standing in front of him, holding a mug of hot coffee. "It's safe," she said, putting it on the table beside him. "I drink only decaf."

He sat up and ran a hand through his curls, embarrassed that she'd caught him nearly napping. "I really ought to hit the road. I don't want to overstay my welcome."

She ignored his comment, and sat cross-legged on the floor in front of a chair exactly like his. "This is my favorite time of day." Elice leaned back, her hair fanning across the cushion.

"Have you lived here long?" he asked.

Elice sat up. "Nearly all my life." She drew up her knees and hugged them to her chest, then rested her chin there. "My folks bought this house when I was in elementary school. I'm an only child, and Mama died when I was ten. Daddy died during my senior year of high school and left me the house and everything in it. Made me quite attractive to certain. . .gentlemen."

A strange, spiteful tone cut into her usually sweet voice. Then, meeting his eyes, she grinned. "I don't know what it is about you. I've told you more about myself tonight than

I've told anyone in a lifetime."

Marge and Helen hadn't looked closely enough at her. They'd described a simple young woman, one so good and decent she didn't even recognize evil when she saw it. He knew better. She not only recognized it, she'd built a barricade to protect herself from it. He knew, because he'd built one exactly like it around his own life.

"I'm curious," she said.

"About what?"

"Why did you become a cop?"

He sipped his coffee. "Lone Ranger Syndrome," he said, smiling. "I believed I could clean up the mean streets. But by the time I grew up enough to see how foolish that ideology was, I was hooked." He took another sip of the coffee. "When Maggie and Lindy died, I had nothing to go home to. So I didn't. Work became my whole life." Cabot sighed.

"And what brought you home?"

He sat forward and firmly planted both big feet on the carpet. "Back to Freeland, you mean?"

Elice nodded.

He shrugged. "Guess I just got sick and tired of death and dying. I wanted to see things grow and live for a change." He sat back again and rested an ankle on a knee, and balanced his coffee cup there. "But enough about me. You said earlier that you never share your troubles with anyone. I just want you to know one thing. . . ." Cabot met her eyes, and held the gaze for a moment before saying, "Ditto."

Elice didn't speak. Instead, she continued looking into his eyes.

The day he met her, he reminded himself he liked 'em tall and blond, blue-eyed and pretty. He'd been suspicious of Elice because nobody, he thought, could be that good. And

she seemed too good to be true. He'd told himself she wasn't
his type. But he'd been wrong. She was his type—exactly.

She stared into space for a long, silent moment, then put
her mug on the table and extended her hand. "If you ever
need a friend, Cabot, you have one, right here."

The moment their fingers entwined, the high wall he'd
built around himself began to crumble. He felt it as surely
as he'd have felt an earthquake. Somehow, this diminutive
woman had shaken his whole world. And she'd done it
with nothing more than a quiet offer of friendship.

two

"Guess I'd better hit the road." Cabot looked at the mantle clock, unable to believe it said eleven-fifteen. "The sign looks great," he added, hoisting it from where she'd leaned it near the front door. "It's going to look terrific at the end of my drive."

Elice felt as though everything stopped as he stood there, looking at her.

"Supper was delicious. I'm glad Annie insisted. . . ."

"We'll do it again sometime," she promised.

"Soon, I hope."

Side by side, they walked to the end of her long, gravel drive, where he'd parked his Jeep. Carefully, he slid the sign into the back seat. "You have a fantastic family," he said, closing the door. "And you're quite a woman, you know that?"

"Cabot. . .stop. You're embarrassing me."

"The truth shouldn't embarrass you, Elice."

He'd never said her name before. Coming from him, it sounded musical, poetic. His face loomed nearer hers, but when his lips made contact, it was with her forehead. Elice pretended she wasn't disappointed.

She watched him climb into the front seat, realizing this tender but tough guy had touched a distant, forgotten chord inside her. He hadn't even left yet, and already she was trying to think of a way to ask him back without appearing overly eager.

Cabot crooked his forefinger, beckoning her near. She

took a step closer to his car door, and he stuck his head out the window. "If you get any weird calls, or if the doorbell rings in the middle of the night, I want you to call me."

She hoped the darkness would hide her blush. "That's not necessary. I shouldn't have bothered you with that—"

"Yes. You should."

"Someone's got their calendar mixed up. They think it's Halloween or something. They'll get bored and stop soon, I'm sure."

"Maybe."

Elice realized he wasn't going to take no for an answer. "I can take care of myself." She said it with conviction and hoped he'd believe her. Because she could, usually.

"It's not a sign of weakness to ask for help, Elice."

Lord, she prayed, *if I had a dollar for every time I heard that since Bobby left, I'd have. . .a couple hundred dollars.*

"So, you have a character flaw after all," he said.

"I beg your pardon?"

"You're stubborn."

She grinned, and wondered how many dollars she could have stacked up for that one. "Perfection is boring."

He reached through the opened window and gently stroked her cheek. "I don't think you're the least bit boring." With that, he winked and backed out of her driveway.

She stood in the driveway, her fingertips resting on the spot he'd touched, until his tail lights were nothing more than tiny red dots in the darkness.

❧

"I want Sugar Pops." Annie stood in the middle of the hallway, rubbing sleep from her eyes.

"Okay, sweetie." Elice hugged her tightly. "Wet or dry today?"

The child put a finger against her pursed lips and gave

the question a moment's thought. "I want my milk in a glass and my cereal dry." Then, grinning impishly, she added, "I'm going to wake up Emi."

"Oh, no, you don't," Elice chided. "You let your sister sleep. Just because you're up with the birds is no reason the rest of the house has to chirp."

Annie followed Elice into the kitchen. "Mommy, do you think Mr. Murray is a nice man?"

Her heart thudded. "Why, yes. I do." *He's a very nice man,* she thought, smiling as she remembered his compliments.

"Then. . .could he be my daddy?"

Her heart pounded harder. "Mr. Murray is a friend. That's all."

"But he doesn't have any kids. He's very lonely. And we need a daddy."

Elice took the cereal box from the pantry shelf and poured golden nuggets into a blue plastic bowl. "You're right. He's lonely. Which is exactly why we're going to be his friends."

She could almost hear the gentle grate of his voice, the deep growl of his laughter. She pictured the shining waves of his hair and his wide, easy smile.

"What's to eat?" Danny asked, stifling a yawn. "I'm starving."

"Sugar Pops," Annie said around a mouthful.

"You're going to turn into a Sugar Pop," he observed. "That's all you ever eat." He turned to Elice. "Can I fry myself an egg, Mom?"

"If you clean up after yourself this time," she said, pouring milk into two plastic cups.

"We're going to be friends with Mr. Murray," Annie announced.

"Good," Danny said. "He's got the best fishing pond

around for miles."

Emily plodded into the kitchen and stretched. "I had the most wonderful dream last night," she sighed dreamily. "Mr. Murray and you got married and we all went to live at Foggy Bottom. I had a big sunny room, and we each got our own pet, and Wally worked for us." She lifted her shoulders in a dainty shrug. "Imagine having a father who looks like a movie star."

"Get real," Danny said, jabbing the egg turner into the egg yolk. "He doesn't look like a movie star. He looks like a quarterback."

"A daddy!" Annie squealed. "Mr. Murray looks like a daddy!"

Emily and Danny exchanged "good grief" glances. "You say that about every man you see," Danny said, rolling his big brown eyes. "I don't want him to be my daddy."

Elice was about to tell Danny he had nothing to worry about, that Cabot Murray certainly didn't want to saddle himself with a frazzled widow and three active kids, when Wally knocked on the back screen door.

"You're early today, Walter," she said, smiling.

"The robins was fightin' up a storm outside my window," he explained, sidestepping into the kitchen, "an' woke me up. They sure can make a racket for such li'l things."

Wally tugged the pockets of his faded army fatigues and shuffled from one booted foot to the other. "What can I do for you today, Miz Glasser?" he asked, combing his fingers through thick, gray curls.

Wally had been helping her ever since Bobby left. He had no family and few friends. People feared him because of his unusual appearance and behavior. But she'd decided long ago to live by The Golden Rule. Where Wally was concerned, it had certainly paid off, for in the five years she'd known him, Elice came to think of him as a fourth child. He looked to her for guidance and comfort, attention and advice.

"I think we'll weed the vegetable garden today," Elice said.

A big, gap-toothed grin split his ruddy face. "I'll get started."

"Not before you have some breakfast, Walter." She pulled out a chair. "How about scrambled eggs and toast?"

"Thanks, Miz Glasser. That would be real nice." He took off his grimy Baltimore Orioles baseball cap. "Did I tell you about my new pet?"

Elice grimaced as he described his latest acquisition. He'd built a cage for it out of soda straws and string, exactly like the ones he'd built for his other "pets." He'd named this bug Happy and had gone to great pains to find the proper diet for his newest insect. Later, as they knelt in the garden, he told her about the job Mr. Olson had given him. "He says he'll give me an extra five dollars a week if I clean out the chicken coops every Saturday. I can buy lots of stuff for my pets with all that extra money."

Before she had a chance to congratulate Wally, Cabot's Jeep pulled into the driveway.

"Hey, Miz Glasser. There's that Murray feller. I heard 'bout him down at the store. They say he ain't very friendly. What do you suppose he's doin' here?"

Elice stood and waved at Cabot. "You can't always believe what you hear, Walter. People don't think Mr. Cozart is a very nice man but I happen to like him." Playfully, she jabbed him in the ribs. "He loves knock-knock jokes."

Wally met her eyes and grinned. "Really?"

The moment Cabot stepped out of the Jeep, her heart began beating doubletime. The closer he got, the faster it beat. He seemed taller, broader, more handsome, if that was possible, dressed in neatly creased jeans and a pale blue shirt.

"Forgot my pictures last night." He'd taken snapshots of his wife and daughter out of his wallet so she could see them better and, in their excitement about a wild pitch during the Orioles' game, forgot all about them.

"They're still on the end table," she said. Then, one hand on Wally's shoulder, she added, "Cabot Murray, I'd like you to meet Walter Hedges. Walter is my right-hand man."

Wally glanced at Elice, his blue eyes filled with pride, then grasped Cabot's extended hand. "She's the only one in town who calls me Walter. Everybody else just calls me Wally."

Elice tucked in one corner of her mouth and overlooked his comment. "Cabot just moved back to Freeland. He lived here when he was a boy."

"I used to live in York. Moved here after the war. Did you leave town to fight in the war?"

"Not exactly. I was a cop. In Chicago."

"Wow." Wally nodded, then held a finger to his temple. "Got shot in Korea. That's why I'm so dumb."

"Walter!" Elice scolded, taking his hand. "You're not dumb, and we all know it."

Beaming at her, he said softly, "Well, you're the only one who feels that way, Miz Glasser, but I sure am glad." For a moment, he stared at their hands, clasped in friendship. He seemed to have more to say. Instead, he dropped to his knees and resumed weeding.

Elice and Cabot chatted for a few more moments before she tapped Wally's shoulder. "You've worked hard enough for one day. Why don't you get out of the hot sun and feed your pets now." When he got to his feet, she added,

"Supper is at six o'clock. We're having roast beef and all the trimmings tonight, and I'd like you to join us."

She'd done it with her usual gentleness, but even Wally knew he'd been dismissed. And he sensed that Cabot was the reason. Leaning close to Elice's ear, without taking his eyes from Cabot's, he whispered, "Watch out for this guy, Miz Glasser. I heard he's mean." With that, he hurried through the backyard and disappeared into the trees.

"Mean?" Cabot repeated, feigning hurt and shock. "Who? Me?"

"He thinks everybody is as honest as he is, so he believes everything he hears," she explained.

"But 'mean?' Where would he hear something like that?"

Elice shrugged and headed for the house. "Why don't you get your pictures while I pour us some lemonade."

He glanced around the yard. "Where are the kids?"

"Inside. Doing their chores."

As they sipped lemonade at her kitchen table, he could hear the sounds of earnest cleaning made by her children above the friendly chatter he shared with Elice. Suddenly, he said, "You sure look pretty today."

She'd dressed hurriedly in old cutoffs and a white tee shirt. Her hair was pulled back in a loose ponytail, and she hadn't put on any makeup. Elice nervously tucked a wisp of hair behind her ear. "Can I get you another ice cube?"

"Your lemonade is perfect," he said, "like everything else about you."

She hid her hands in her lap, one repeatedly squeezing the other, and flushed in response to his compliment.

Cabot touched her cheek. "You're really cute when you do that. Last time I saw a woman blush, it was my mother-in-law. . .and she was having a hot flash." He laughed heartily. "I didn't stick around to see how long it lasted, but I'd

sure like to be here when yours fades." His thumb drew
tiny circles on her jaw.

Elice didn't know which she liked more, the sound of his
laughter or the feel of his warm skin against hers. She sensed
something in this man, something good and decent. Elice
hadn't been mindfully advertising for a relationship, but suddenly, she realized that Cabot had applied for the job. One
thing was certain: It was wonderful to feel like a whole
woman again.

"So your birthday is coming up, eh?"

Nodding, she wished she'd never given him that information.

"In that case, I'm going home to get some work done,
and then I'm coming back here to take you out to dinner. I
want to be the first to help you celebrate. What's your pref-
erence? Italian? French? Chinese?"

She swallowed. "It's sweet of you to ask," she began,
"but I couldn't possibly—"

"Why not?"

He reminded her of Danny, sitting there, wide-eyed and
expectant. She hated saying no—for herself as much as for
him. But she couldn't go out with him. The only people
who'd ever cared for the kids in her absence were Bobby's
parents. And how could she ask them to babysit their son's
children while she dated another man!

"Because I don't have a sitter."

He sighed. "Is that all? I thought you were going to say
you don't like ex-cops or something." Cabot laughed. "The
more the merrier, I always say."

"No. That's out of the question. I couldn't ask you
to—"

"You're not asking. I am."

"But—"

"But nothing. Think of it as a 'Welcome Cabot Back to Freeland' celebration if it makes you feel better."

He sat in silence for a long time, his hazel eyes glowing. "I hate to eat alone. Especially when I'm celebrating." He squeezed her hand. "So, what do you say?"

"Say to what?" Danny asked, returning the kitchen trash can to its proper place under the sink.

"A potential ally!" Cabot said, slapping his muscular thigh. Then, focusing on the boy, he added, "I'm trying to talk your mother into letting me treat you guys to dinner. To celebrate her birthday. Help me convince her to say 'Yes.'"

Danny's dark eyes moved from his mother's face to the man's. "Well, there are plenty of things I'd rather do," he began, his voice sullen, "but Mom deserves a treat." He grinned at Elice. "I think we should do it."

"Should do what?" Emily asked her brother as she joined them in the kitchen.

"Mr. Murray wants to take us all out to dinner to celebrate Mom's birthday."

"Oh, Mr. Murray," Emily sighed and clasped her hands in front of her chest. "What a wonderful idea! Can we get all dressed up?"

"Dressed up for what?" Annie wanted to know, climbing onto Elice's lap.

"Mr. Murray's going to take us all out. . .a birthday party for Mom," Danny explained for the second time.

"If I didn't know better," Elice said, smiling, "I'd say this whole thing was a conspiracy."

"Does that mean yes?" Cabot leaned forward as he asked the question.

"Please?" Annie whined.

"It would be so romantic," Emily gushed.

Danny hesitated, then said, "It might be fun."

Elice shook her head and held up her hands in mock sur-
render. "Okay. All right. I give up. We'll go."

"You're terrific, Mom," Emily said, hugging her.

Laugh lines crinkled around his cinnamon-colored eyes.
"Yeah, Mom. You're terrific."

"I suppose you're going to make me wear a tie," Danny
complained, following Cabot to the front door.

"Not only that, but you're all going to stop calling me
'Mr. Murray,' too." He looked each child in the eye and
grinned. "I want you to call me Cabot from now on. Got
that?"

The children nodded and returned his smile.

Wally heard them coming and didn't want Elice to know
he hadn't obeyed when she had told him to go home. He'd
never deliberately displeased her and didn't want to start
now, so he hid behind the big oak tree in her front yard.

"See you at six," Cabot called from the Jeep.

Four smiling faces stared out the picture window. Four
hands waved goodbye. Four hearts beat a little faster. . .
especially the biggest heart.

❧

He'd been surprising them with visits nearly every day since
the birthday outing. And every time he did, Cabot brought
little treats for the children. He'd hear none of Elice's
objections, insisting that since he had no children of his own
to spoil, it was her duty to let him spoil hers. The girls
squealed with delight when he pulled hair ribbons or col-
ored pencils from his shirt pocket. And Danny, though he
tried to portray an "I don't care" attitude, grinned when
Cabot produced a fishing lure or a box of shiny aluminum
hooks.

Cabot and the kindnesses he performed seemed to pop
into her mind at the strangest moments. As she watered the

Swedish ivy plant he'd given her for her birthday, she smiled.

"Mom! Come out here!" Danny's excited voice continued, "Hurry, Mom. You're not gonna believe this."

She dried her hands on the dish towel and went outside and found Danny beside her old yellow Vega, pointing at its tires. "What's goin' on, Mom?"

Elice couldn't believe her eyes. In all the years she'd lived in Freeland, nothing like this had ever happened. She tried to formulate an explanation that would satisfy her frightened son, but nothing made sense.

"Oh no," Emily said, hugging Elice's arm. "Did you run over a bunch of nails or something?"

Elice walked around the car, then bent down to inspect the tires. "I suppose that's possible," she said, feeling around for sharp objects. "But nothing seems to be sticking out."

When she heard his Jeep roar up the drive, she thought she knew how the early settlers felt when they heard the distant notes of the cavalry's bugle. It amazed her how he showed up, just when she needed him most, as if he could read her mind.

"Good morning," he called, smiling. "How's every—" His greeting and his grin died the moment he saw her tires. "What happened?"

"They were fine last night when I took the kids into Shrewsbury for ice cream," Elice said.

Cabot frowned at her, then at the car. He moved in for a closer look. "Just as I suspected," he said, running his fingers along the black rubber, "punctures."

The word frightened her. Broken glass, nails, anything else could have been chalked up to an accident. But punctures, with no telltale evidence, meant someone had deliberately done this. But who? And why?

She saw Cabot's eyes travel to each of her children's

worried faces. "Probably some smart aleck teenager pulling a silly prank," he said, forcing a grin. "Say, kids, I've got something for you. On the front seat. Why don't you bring it here."

Immediately, their faces lit up and they ran toward his vehicle. "Strawberries!" they shouted from inside the jeep. "A whole big box of them!"

"Why don't you take them inside and rinse them off," Elice suggested as they ran toward her and Cabot, "and I'll make some strawberry shortcake for dessert tonight."

The minute the kids were out of sight, she turned her back to the kitchen window, so they wouldn't be able to read the worried look on her face. "This makes no sense, Cabot."

"You'll drive yourself crazy trying to figure out why anybody would do a thing like this. The world is full of loonies and nuts." He pointed at the tires. "You don't need much more proof than that."

She took a deep breath and stood tall. "You're right. What I need to concentrate on right now is getting them replaced. My father always saved the most peculiar things; I seem to recall tires in the shed. I only hope they're the right size." Elice headed for the small, wooden building that sat at the far end of her property.

"Let me do it for you," he said, grabbing her elbow.

"I was hoping you'd say that," she teased. "And when you're finished, I'll fix you a nice big lunch."

"Can't think of anything I'd rather do."

It took him half an hour to get all four tires changed. Cabot was wiping his grimy hands on the old rag she kept in the shed as he joined her in the kitchen. "Where does this Wally character live?"

She frowned, immediately understanding his insinuation. "Walter didn't do it."

He raised his hands defensively. "I'm not accusing him." Cabot continued to run the rag over his hands. "I remember the way he looked at you when I was over here the other day. He's very. . .fond of you."

She lifted her chin in stubborn defiance. "Walter has been a good friend to us since Bobby died. I don't know what we would have done without him."

Cabot tucked the rag into his back pocket, then crossed both arms over his chest. "Is he here a lot?"

"Several times a week." She took a loaf of bread from its drawer.

"He doesn't have a job?"

Elice placed ten slices on the counter, then slapped a piece of bologna onto each. "He does odds and ends at the Olsons' in exchange for the use of a shack out back."

"How does he feed and clothe himself?"

"He gets a pension. 'Bandage money' he calls it." She paused in the spreading of mustard. "You're beginning to sound like Kojak again, and this time, I don't like it one bit."

He'd been hounding her like a spoiled child, and she'd talked to him as if that's exactly what he was. He looked so surprised at her tone that it made her grin.

"Look. What are we making such a big deal about?" she asked. "It's four flat tires, not the end of the world."

Cabot only stood there grinning.

"I know he seems strange," she admitted, filling five glasses with lemonade, "but Walter wouldn't hurt a fly." Laughing, she added, "I mean that literally. He's adopted several, you know."

His brows knitted.

"He collects bugs. Names them. Builds little cages for them and feeds them. If you could see how lovingly—"

"Uh. . .Elice," he said, "I mean no disrespect, but that's . . .that's just plain weird."

Sighing, she looked at the ceiling. *Please God*, she prayed, *help me make him understand.* "But don't you see?" she began. "If Walter could be kind to a bug, of all things, he couldn't possibly hurt me." She giggled again. "Why, I've baked him brownies—"

"Would he know it if he hurt you? I mean. . .could he have flattened the tires because they made a neat sound?"

The maternal frown returned to her brow as she shook her head. "If you could only hear how ridiculous you sound." Elice sighed again. "Look," she began, "Walter is slow, but he isn't stupid. Nor is he mean."

Cabot pocketed both hands. It was all well and good to believe in people, but Elice carried the idea to a dangerous extreme. "Now you look," he said, no longer caring if she heard the anger in his voice. "Wally may be abnormal by some standards, but he's still a man. And he's been bitten by the Green-Eyed Monster. It's as plain as the mustard on your spoon."

She glanced at the utensil, then dropped it noisily into the sink.

A warm light beamed from his hazel eyes as he took her hands in his. "He's not stupid. . .you've got that right." He took a step closer, and drew her into a warm, protective hug. "He has excellent taste, too."

ಎ

Wally liked this spot under her kitchen window. The shrub was tall and thick, and shaded him from the blistering afternoon sun. It was a good place to hide. Sometimes, he'd sit there for hours, listening to her pretty voice, enjoying the happy banter of her kids. He'd spent many afternoons that way. It was almost as good as having the fun himself.

He'd accepted his limitations. Learned to live with what he'd become. Occasionally, though, in more lucid moments, he remembered what he'd been like before Korea. Before the head injury, when he'd had a fiancée and a good job and a nice apartment in York, Pennsylvania. Wally didn't dwell on those days, though, for the memory of them made a mean mood grow inside him. A stormy, scary feeling, so powerful that he sometimes worried he might do something. . .bad.

Dark clouds formed in his head as he sat quietly in the dirt behind the bush. That big cop is trying to blame all the bad things on me, he realized. He's trying to get Miz Glasser to think I'm the one who's been doing scary things to her.

She was the most important person in his life, followed only by her children, who called him Big Buddy Wally. At the Glassers' he'd always been treated like family. . .with respect. They were his only real friends. He liked Cabot just fine—as long as he didn't tamper with that—

But Wally had a dream: That someday, Elice would see him as a man, a real man.

❧

"It hurts, Mom," Danny complained.

In less than an hour, she'd unintentionally harmed all three of her children. First, she'd caught Emily's back in a zipper. Then, she'd pulled too hard making Annie's ponytail. And now she was choking her only son with a blue silk tie.

"You look terrific, Mom," Emily said, hugging her from behind.

Elice hadn't paid a lot of attention to her appearance these past few years. But lately, because she never knew when Cabot might drop by, Elice always tried to look her best. "Do you really think so?"

"Aw, Mom. You're gorgeous. And if he doesn't think so, he's a big dumb jerk." Danny was still having a bit of trouble accepting the fact that Cabot could never replace him in Elice's life. She knew he liked the big guy, yet the boy never resisted an opportunity to put him in his place which, in Danny's opinion, was anywhere but near his mother. Elice was about to scold Danny for his disrespectful remark when Annie's excited voice stopped her.

"He's here!" the little girl announced, jumping up and down.

Elice closed her eyes for a moment, tilted her face to the heavens, and took a deep breath. *I'm in Your hands,* she prayed silently. *Please don't let me say anything stupid, or trip, or spill anything in my lap.*

It didn't matter that she'd seen him nearly every day for the past month. Or that this hadn't been the first time they'd gone to dinner. Though they rarely had a moment alone, she had to admit that this dating stuff wasn't as easy as it had been with Bobby.

"Hello, there," Cabot said from his side of the screen door.

The gray suit accented his deep tan and made his pale eyes look more golden than ever.

"I wonder if you'd do me a favor," she said, holding the door open for him. "I'm afraid the authorities are going to prosecute me for child abuse if someone doesn't help Danny with his tie."

Cabot tried not to laugh at Danny's pinched expression. "I'd be honored," he said, his fingertips brushing her cheek. "Come here, Dan," he said. Turning the boy around, he worked from behind and taught him how to tie a perfect Windsor knot. "Guess since I'm responsible for your having to wear one of these things every week or so, the least I can do is teach you how to tie one."

Danny's eyes widened as he realized what he'd done all by himself. "Hey. That wasn't so hard. Look, Mom. I did it myself!"

She smiled. "You look very handsome. And very grown up."

Danny faced Cabot. "I polished my shoes again. Just like for Mom's birthday dinner—"

"Blinding!" Cabot said, shading his eyes from an imaginary glare.

He focused on Emily, then, who stood quietly near the door, her hands folded primly in front of her pale blue dress. She had the loveliest golden hair he'd ever seen, and he told her so. "One of these days, you're going to break a lot of hearts."

She blushed and grinned and stared at her white sandals.

"Hey! What about me?" Annie pouted.

Cabot made note of Annie's frilly lavender dress. "Darlin', you're as pretty as a baby duck."

She gave his comment a moment's thought. Then, hands on her hips and a frown on her face, she said, "Mommy, are baby ducks pretty?"

"All babies are pretty, sweetie."

Cabot pocketed his hands and took a quick inventory of Elice's attire. "You're going to break some hearts, too," he said softly. "Probably mine."

On the way to the restaurant, Annie leaned over the front seat and pointed. "Mommy, look. . .rides!"

"Tell you what," Cabot said. "You'd only get your pretty dress all dirty if we went to the carnival on the way home. So how about if we go tomorrow night?"

Three gasps echoed in the back seat.

"Cabot, you're spoiling us. We can't let you keep—"

"There's something you ought to know about me, pretty lady," he said. "Nobody lets me do anything." Reaching across the space between them, he grabbed her hand. "You'd

better wear your sneakers and jeans tomorrow night, kids,"
he said over his shoulder, "'cause I like the wild rides."

"That makes one of us," Elice muttered, giving in to his
whim.

"You mean. . .that makes four of us," Danny countered.

⁂

After he brought them home, Cabot sat on the back porch
as Elice tucked the children in for the night. When she
joined him, she carried two glasses of lemonade.

"I hope you don't mind my constant intrusion into your
life," he said, once she'd settled into the chair beside him.

"Intrusion?" she asked. "I'd hardly call you an intrusion."

"What would you call me, then?"

Elice leaned her head against the back of the chair and
squinted as she considered her answer. "I guess I'd have to
say you're a very pleasant diversion."

"From what?"

"Everything."

"Hmmm," he said. And after a moment, he said it again.
"Hmmm."

She liked the sound of his voice and the way he behaved
with her children. She liked his sense of humor and the
easy smile that seemed reserved for the Glasser family alone.
"Do you believe this sky?" she asked, hoping to change the
subject. "And they were calling for a thunderstorm."

"Let's hope it's this starry tomorrow night."

She stole a quick peek at his profile. "The kids will be
disappointed if it rains. We didn't get to go to the carnival
last year."

"I'll be disappointed, too. How 'bout you?"

Again she took her time answering. "I'd hate for it to
rain."

He sat forward, leaned his elbows on his knees, and

clasped his hands. "Elice, I think you know me well enough by now to realize I'm not a man who minces words." He stared at an invisible spot between his polished cowboy boots. "I like you. I like you a lot." He cleared his throat, then met her eyes. "And I think you like me, too. At least," he said, grinning, "I sure hope you do."

Coughing, he shook his head. "So. . .would you mind very much if I. . .if I kissed you?"

She remembered how disappointed she'd been that first night, when he hadn't kissed her goodbye. Ever since then, she'd been hoping to find out if his lips would feel as warm and wonderful as she thought they might.

"We haven't known each other very long," he said slowly, "but then, we're not children anymore. We don't. . . ."

He moved in the chair, wincing when it squeaked. "I don't want to do or say anything that would. . .I mean. . . ." He combed his fingers through his hair. "What I'm trying to say is that I don't want you to get away. But I don't want to scare you away, either."

"You don't scare me," she said, quietly and without hesitation.

He stood and held his hand out to her. Immediately, she took it, and they walked the perimeter of her two-acre yard, discussing everything from politics to pelicans. Without warning, he put himself in her path. "Do you have any idea what you do to me?"

She looked up at him, the dim light of the quarter moon reflected in her dark eyes.

"It took a while, after Maggie, but eventually I got back on the old horse, so to speak. But those women I dated. . . . They were. . . ." He glanced around her hard, as if the ending to his sentence hung on a tree branch or nestled in a bush. "You're more beautiful on the inside than you are on the outside. And believe me, that's saying a mouthful."

She laughed softly. "Do you enjoy embarrassing me?"

"No more than you enjoy making me repeat myself. The truth shouldn't embarrass you, Elice."

They walked a few more steps before he added, "It wasn't so long ago that I believed I'd never get close to a woman again." He cupped her chin, tilted her face until their eyes met. "Do you believe in love at first sight?"

Cabot watched her as he continued, "I guess I sound certifiable to you. I've known you only a couple of months and already I'm talking about love." His laughter floated across the dew-sparkled yard. "You want to hear something even funnier? I've never felt more sane. . .nor more certain of anything in my life."

He stopped talking then and stopped laughing. His face moved closer to hers. So near that it blurred before her eyes. Strong arms slipped around her, drawing her to him, so that not even the warm summer breeze could have passed between them. Moonlight and starlight and the glitter of dew glowed around them as they embraced, as if God Himself had blessed their embrace.

It had been a long time since anything had touched her so deeply. The heart whose only function, moments ago, had been to keep her alive, now pumped furiously with a whole new purpose. He kissed the tip of her nose, her forehead, her chin. "We'll take our time," he promised, hugging her tightly. "I have the rest of my life. How 'bout you?"

She felt herself relax in his arms, and nodded against his chest.

"Is there any more lemonade?" he asked.

"I think I can squeeze one more glass from the pitcher."

Hand in hand, they headed back to the porch. "I've been thinking. . . ."

"Uh-oh," she teased. "I smell trouble."

"I'll just ignore that," he said, giving her a sideways hug. "What I was thinking? How would you feel about redecorating my house?"

She stood still and stared up at him.

"Don't give me that 'why me' look. I've seen what you can do. Your place is wonderful. I want that kind of warmth where I live, too."

She lifted her chin and grinned. "I've always wanted to be a designer."

"Then you'll take the job?"

Giggling, she said, "Job. You make it sound like—"

"I couldn't let you do it for free."

"'Nobody lets me do anything,'" she quoted.

He held up a hand to silence her. "Touché. But you already have enough to do. You can't do it for nothing."

"I wouldn't be doing it for nothing," she said. "I'd be doing it for a friend."

The simplicity of her statement silenced him, and wiped the silly grin from his face. "Friend?" Cabot put his hands on her shoulders and drew her near. "I'd like to be a whole lot more than just your friend, Elice."

Every cell in her body applauded his statement. Enough time had passed since she'd buried Bobby. It was time to begin again. And she felt certain that God would approve. She smiled slightly, imagining God, casually leaning on the Golden Gate, forming the Victory sign, like Winston Churchill.

"What's so funny?" he wanted to know.

"Nothing," she said, and slipped her arms around him. "I'm just wondering if you're ever going to kiss me."

Brawny arms held her tightly as his lips covered hers. A quiet groan echoed deep in his chest. "Mmm-mmm," he growled. "You sure taste fine, pretty lady."

"Like lemonade?"

He nodded. "Mmmm. And I'm very thirsty."

three

How could Cabot have known that Elice would wear what he had: jeans and boots and a red gingham shirt? They endured the gentle teasing of her kids, knowing full well that anyone who saw them at the carnival would assume their attire had been a calculated, if not silly, plan. Still, it pleased him that they thought so much alike.

While Elice and the children waited in the long line to ride the ferris wheel, Cabot got in another line to purchase tickets.

"Well, looky here," said a deep, gravelly voice. "If it ain't pretty little Leecie." A heavy hand rested on her shoulder. "Why, I haven't seen you in a coon's age."

Elice turned in time to see Jack Wilson ruffle Danny's hair. The boy grimaced and used his fingers to comb his dark locks back into place.

"Whatcha been up to, Leecie?" he asked, dark eyes canvassing her. "I'll say this for you. . .you look fine, mighty fine."

For as long as she'd known Jack Wilson, he'd managed the Hickory Ridge Cannery. She liked him. He'd always treated her with kindness and respect. As far as she could tell, he had two faults: He was a chain smoker and he couldn't take "No" for an answer. For some time now he'd been after Elice to be his girl. But Jack wasn't her type. Not then and certainly not now that she'd met Cabot.

"It's good to see you, Jack. How have you been?"

"Missin' you," was his simple response.

She couldn't tell if he was winking flirtatiously or merely squinting around the cigarette smoke that encircled his head.

He focused on Emily. "Look at you. Aren't you gettin' pretty?" Jack whistled when he looked at Annie. "Looks like you've grown a foot taller since I last saw you."

Both girls smiled shyly, then pretended to be engrossed in watching the ride. Danny, on the other hand, glared at him openly.

"Here we go," Cabot sang, flapping the tickets. "I got us three books. That way I won't have to stand in that mob anymore and—"

Jack turned, looked from Cabot's shirt to Elice's, and back again. Understanding registered on his weathered, mustachioed face. "Well, Leecie. It's about time, I gotta say. Even if I'd rather you'd chosen me."

Cabot stuck out his hand in friendly greeting and pumped his former schoolmate's arm. "What have you been up to, you old dog?" he asked, grinning.

Jack shrugged. "Working hard. Hardly working. Depends on your point of view," he said, grinding the cigarette into the gravel as he grinned back. But the smile died when he said through clenched teeth, "I was real sorry to hear about Maggie."

Cabot swallowed. *So. It's still like that, is it?* He recalled now what he'd always disliked about Jack: Whatever Cabot had, Jack wanted. He'd wanted to be first string on their high school football team, but skipped practices and broke curfew so often the coach dropped him from the roster. And he'd wanted Cabot's red '67 Chevy; if Jack had worked twenty hours a week, as Cabot had, he could have had one just like it. All through high school, Jack considered Maggie his girl, even though she'd repeatedly said they were just friends.

When Cabot had picked up Maggie at Chicago's O'Hare Airport the day before their wedding, she told him how Jack had followed her to Baltimore's terminal, tearfully pleading for her to stay. He'd promised to be the best husband a woman ever had, if she'd only stay with him in Freeland. She'd heard him say, as she boarded the plane, that someday Cabot would pay for stealing her. For weeks, it bothered Maggie that Jack had been hurt, even if it had only been because of his stubborn refusal to accept facts. Eventually, Cabot convinced her that Jack would soon get over it. He'd marry and have kids, and forget that either of them existed.

But Jack had never married, and he certainly hadn't forgotten that Cabot and Maggie existed.

"Looks like you win again," Jack was saying.

Elice looked from Jack's face to Cabot's, her eyes wide and frightened as she tried to understand the reason for the boiling fury in Jack's eyes.

"Any competition between you and me has always been a figment of your imagination, old buddy, and you know it." Cabot's eyes glowed like hot coals, despite his cool words and careful smile.

Jack shrugged off Cabot's retort and draped a tanned arm across Elice's shoulders. "Well, all I can say is that this is one special lady, fella, and you'd better treat her right." He paused, his dark eyes glittering dangerously, as he lit another cigarette and inhaled deeply before adding, " 'Cause if something like what happened to Maggie should happen to little Leecie, here, you're going to answer to me."

Jack's dark eyes gleamed with quiet longing. Then, hugging Elice, he said, "You deserve to be happy. Just don't let yourself settle for less than the best." He dropped a brotherly kiss on her cheek, and walked away.

"What was that all about?" she asked Cabot when Jack was out of earshot. She'd never seen him so angry.

"Don't pay any attention to him," Cabot said. "Jack's been a hothead all his life, and it's gotten him into trouble more times than I care to remember." Then, he noticed the somber, frightened faces of her kids and, to lighten the atmosphere, said, "How are we going to work this out, guys? There are five of us, and they allow only three to a seat up there." He gestured to the highest seat on the big ferris wheel.

"You ride with Mom," Danny said, jabbing his thumb against his chest, "and I'll take care of the girls."

"Now that's what I call an idea, Dan!"

The boy grinned and mimicked Cabot, planting his feet a shoulder's width apart and crossing his arms over his chest. "Know what I like about you?"

"What?" Cabot asked, grinning back.

"You never mess up my hair, and you don't call me 'Danny.' I'm too old for that kind of stuff." He peeked at his mother. "But you can still call me 'Danny,' Mom."

"I'm hurt, kiddo," Cabot said, poking his shoulder. "And here I thought you liked me 'cause I'm such a fun guy."

Danny snickered. "You're okay, I guess."

Cabot patted the boy's back. "And you're okay, too, Dan."

"What about me?" Annie wanted to know.

Cabot lifted her high into the air. "Darlin'," he said, kissing her cheek, "I adore you." Putting her back onto the ground, he gently touched Emily's cheek. "You, too, kiddo."

Cabot slipped an arm around Elice's waist, his lips fractions of an inch from her ear. "But just between you and me," he whispered conspiratorially, "I like you best."

❧

She plopped into a lawn chair and sighed. "They're finally

tucked in." Grinning, she turned to him. "When was the last time you settled in after a long hard day. . .with a tall glass of grape Kool-Aid?"

One blond brow rose as he pursed his lips. "It's been a long time. In fact, it's been. . . . Why, I don't believe I've had grape Kool-Aid in my entire life."

They laughed as a roll of thunder sounded in the distance.

"Looks like we're finally going to get that storm they've been promising all week," she said.

"Wonder if it's gonna be an all-nighter?"

"I suppose if it rains tomorrow, the picnic at Foggy Bottom is off."

"My porch has a roof, too, you know."

She shrugged. "Then I guess it depends on which way the wind is blowing."

"It wouldn't dare rain on our barbecue."

As if on cue, the wind kicked up and the thunder echoed closer. A bolt of lightning cracked nearby, brightening the entire yard.

"That breeze feels good." She closed her eyes.

"Smells good, too."

"I like night rain. Puts me right to sleep." She sensed that the atmosphere had changed abruptly, and opened her eyes to see why. The reason was simple: Cabot was on his knees, leaning on the arm of her lawn chair, his smiling face just inches from hers. Gently, he kissed her.

Chuckling, he said, "You don't have a romantic bone in your body. You're supposed to close your eyes when I do that."

She closed her eyes and puckered up. And she stayed that way until he'd given her another sweet kiss.

"You're perfect for me," he said.

Silence was her only response.

"What's going on in that pretty head of yours?"

"Well, you were right when you said we're not children, but. . . ."

He sat back on his heels, his gruff yet tender chuckle telling her he understood. "Moving a little too fast for you, am I?" He squeezed her hand. "I'm a man of my word," he said, adding, "We'll take our time." Cabot pulled her into a standing position and hugged her.

Her fingers combed through the soft blond waves that touched his shirt collar. "Thanks for understanding, Cabot."

"A kiss is just a kiss," he sang into her ear. And his next kiss came at the exact moment as a violent clap of thunder. She couldn't be sure which had caused the furious beating of her heart—nature in the sky or nature in her arms.

"Mommy," Annie whimpered, "I'm scared."

The spell shattered, they turned toward the sleepy, frightened child. Something deep inside him ached. Lindy had been afraid of thunder, too. In fact, one of his last fatherly functions had been to comfort her during a storm.

"I'll just rock her back to sleep," she said. "I won't be long."

"Let me. . . ." He carried Annie into the house. "How about we sit in Mommy's chair, and I'll sing you some lullabies."

Annie nestled her face in the crook of his neck and nodded. Less than an hour later, Elice took the sleeping child from his arms and carefully put her back into bed. When she returned, Cabot was fast asleep in the chair, his long legs outstretched and his big hands folded on his chest. Long pale lashes curved upward from his cheekbones as the peace of deep slumber softened the face that, during the daytime, tried so hard to appear cop-hard.

She couldn't wake him, only to send him into a raging

thunderstorm. Instead, Elice draped a crisp, line-dried sheet over him and turned out the lights. After one last peek at his boyish position in her chair, she tiptoed into her room.

ک

He woke to the trilling of the phone, and spoke a groggy "Hello" into the mouthpiece.

Her husky voice said, "I hate to bother you, Cabot, but since you were a policeman, I thought. . . ."

He'd never heard fear in her voice before. Not when she spoke about the phone calls. Not when she mentioned the doorbell business. Not even when her tires had been slashed. The fact that she'd lost her usual composure at all scared him. "I'll be right there," he promised.

Keep away from the cop or you'll be sorry, said the note she handed him the moment he walked through the door. It had been typed on the same machine as the note he'd found on his kitchen table. He knew because the *e* was slightly askew. Whoever delivered it had even used the same blue stationery. Cabot tried to keep his hands still as he reread the note. "Where did you find this?"

"It was on the kitchen table when I got up this morning . . .right beside your note."

He remembered the message he'd scribbled on the back of an envelope, using a fat orange crayon to explain that when he woke and couldn't get back to sleep, he'd decided to leave. . .to protect her reputation. But he'd miss her, he wrote, and would call her first thing in the morning. Cabot's hand trembled with anger as he held the threatening message. If he hadn't been so concerned about public opinion, he'd have been there when this lunatic showed up. Perhaps he could have prevented this.

"Did you lock the door before you went to bed?" he asked, suddenly.

"Of course I did. Didn't you have to unlock it to get out?"

Yes. And he'd made sure to lock it behind him, too.

"What about the window?" Cabot walked toward the sink to inspect the lock on the window.

"Everything was fine. Normal. Until I found that." It may as well have been a rattlesnake coiled for attack, the way she looked at the note in his hand.

"Well, whoever wrote it got in through here," he said, indicating the black scuff mark on the kitchen counter. "He pried open the window and stepped right on in."

Her hands flew to her face. For a moment, she shuddered. But almost immediately, she squared her shoulders and got hold of herself. "I'm going to put on a pot of coffee."

"Good. I could use a cup." One hand on the back doorknob, he stuffed the note into his shirt pocket. "I'm going outside to have a look around."

Elice nodded and sent him a trembly smile.

He couldn't stand to see her this way. Cabot gave her a little hug. "You okay?"

Again she nodded. But this time, she made an effort to look brave and strong. He hesitated, not wanting to leave her alone, not even for the few minutes it would take to have a look around outside. He was under the kitchen window when he heard the kids' voices. Emily and Danny were debating between scrambled eggs and Cocoa Puffs, and Annie wanted Sugar Pops. He found several large footprints and one handprint pressed into the red clay dirt. There were smudges on the white window frame, and a few more on the pane itself.

The voice that lived inside him, offering warnings and advice, began to speak. It whispered three names, and Deitrich headed the list. But it wasn't like Deitrich to pull dumb pranks. Pull a trigger, yes, but taunt a widow with notes and phone calls? Deitrich was too savvy a crook for that. And Freeland was too small a town for a "strike now, pay later" guy like him.

Or was it? Maybe he was thinking precisely what Deitrich wanted him to think.

On second thought, Cabot decided to call the police from Foggy Bottom, to keep the kids from overhearing the report. Then he'd come back to Twin Acres and wait. For the first time in his life, he regretted Freeland's rural setting; the Baltimore County police were a full thirty minutes away.

Cabot went back inside and pulled Elice into the living room. "Get the kids out of here," he said. "Take 'em to York. Go shopping at the mall. See a movie. Whatever. There's no sense in getting them all riled up. This could be nothing." But he knew better. And so did she. He could see it in her wide, frightened eyes.

"All right, Cabot. I'll leave. But only if you promise not to keep anything from me. I don't need to be protected, you know. I'm a big girl. I've been on my own a long time. This is my house, after all, and I deserve to hear the truth."

She stood there, chin up and shoulders back, toughing it out, just as she'd toughed out other difficulties in her life. The difference, he decided, was that this time she didn't have to go it alone. Because he'd be there, right beside her, every step of the way.

Suddenly, it struck him that it was because of him that she was going through this whole ordeal in the first place. Spontaneously, he hugged her again. Only then did he notice the trembling in her body. "It'll be all right," he soothed. "I'll make it all right."

❧

He wandered alone through the quiet rooms of her house, waiting for the police to arrive. A place for everything, everything in its place, save a toy here or there to indicate the presence of children. Elice took as much care of her home as she did of her kids, her business, her gardens.

The black scuff on the counter throbbed its presence in the otherwise perfect room, just as the note on the table shouted its existence into the otherwise peaceful atmosphere. The more thought he gave the matter, the more certain he was that someone was trying to get at him through Elice.

And it was working, too. He'd never been more terrified in his life. Not in dark Chicago alleys, where armed robbers hid. Not in dank apartments, where drug dealers did their dirty business. The things that had been going on at Foggy Bottom were unnerving, unsettling. But he could handle that. He'd had his share of self-defense battles over the years and had managed to come through each alive and well.

This was different, completely different. The phone calls and mysterious nonpresence at her door had been tiny warnings. So had the tire incident. But to have entered her home while she and the children slept. . . . The thought chilled Cabot to the bone. Whoever had been terrorizing her had stopped playing games; he was serious now.

Cabot ached, deep inside. He'd almost given up hope of ever living a normal life again. . .until Elice. He'd resigned himself to being alone, without children—until her kids. They were his now, in his heart, anyway. He wondered what he'd done to anger God this time. Why else would this be happening now, when he'd come so close to happiness again?

Once the officers arrived, explaining the situation took very little time, much to his surprise. By his recollection, it seemed to take witnesses hours to tell even the simplest stories. Being on the other end of the investigation, he realized that time moves differently when you're the victim.

As the uniformed officers wrote down the facts as Cabot knew them, he realized how vague and useless the information would be. He knew long before they admitted it aloud that the cops were helpless and frustrated. Without concrete evidence, their hands were tied. They left, saying they'd cruise the area several times a day. More than that, they couldn't promise.

Well, then, Cabot decided, I'll just have to pick up the slack. He'd find the evidence the police needed. He wouldn't rest until he had enough proof to allow them to make an arrest that would stick. Because he wanted whoever was doing this to Elice locked up for a long, long time.

&

"New locks?" Elice repeated. "What good will that do? He didn't even come in through the door!"

Through some miracle he didn't quite understand—or feel he deserved—she'd agreed to come with him to Foggy Bottom. "I can use the time to get started on this redecorating project," she said, stacking the cans of paint and boxes of brushes and rollers she'd brought from her workshop in a corner of Cabot's kitchen.

"I'll pay for the locks. It's just a precaution."

"It's not the money, and you know it. You've got it into your head that this is your fault. And it isn't. Locks can't change that fact."

But he was to blame. If he'd listened to his gut, he'd never become involved with her in the first place. He should have known that threats and violence would follow him wherever he went. And it was killing him that he'd brought it right into her house.

Elice sighed. "You're the most exasperating man, Cabot Murray. Do you honestly think you were such a great cop that every criminal you put behind bars spends every waking moment thinking up ways to get even with you?"

Great cop? he thought. A deep furrow formed on his forehead and his mouth became a taut line. "This has nothing to do with my ego, Elice," he snapped. "I don't need an anti-machismo speech from you right now."

Her left brow lifted. "You're a gentleman, so naturally, you'll listen to anything I have to say." She took a step closer, put her hands on her hips, and narrowed her eyes. "And I say you're not responsible for what's been happening."

Cabot shook his head. "You're the one who's exasperating," he said. "You think you have a direct connection to heaven and God tells you how things are. Well, you're naive. That's what you are."

It was a low blow and he knew it. But Cabot had to make her realize that their relationship had been a mistake. That it had to end—now. Before the note-delivering lunatic got it into his head to do something really dangerous, something violent.

She took a deep breath, and another step closer. "Did the police have anything else to say? Or was 'Get new locks' all the professional advice they had to offer?"

He couldn't believe her. She had more spunk than most men he knew. Somehow, she'd gotten it into her head that everything could be rationalized and explained with one Bible verse or another. What would it take to wise her up . . .death? The moment the word entered his head, his heart thudded wildly in his chest. The very idea terrified him. He looked at her, standing there, not two feet from him, hands on her hips and fire in her eyes. He wanted to take her in his arms and tell her how sorry he was. But he didn't dare. "Do you have any idea how gorgeous you are when you're all fired up like that?" he said. "For two cents, I'd kiss the living daylights out of you, right where you stand."

Her mouth dropped open as her eyes widened. Elice reached into her jeans pocket, withdrew two pennies, and tossed them at his feet. "Put your money where your mouth is, Mr. Murray," she said, grinning.

He couldn't help himself. Cabot laughed, soft and slow at first. "I'm sorry," he said, wrapping her in his arms. "I didn't mean to bark at you. It's just that. . . ." He kissed the top of her head. "You don't seem to realize how serious this is. There's a crazy person out there with a fantasy to fulfill. You and the kids could be in real danger."

"What do you take me for," she fumed, pulling out of his embrace, "some kind of addle-brained twit? I understand the seriousness of this situation. What I don't understand is why you blame yourself."

Cabot released a long, whispering sigh, closed his eyes, and shook his head. "I feel like a tape recorder. We went all through this earlier." He faced her, his feet planted wide on the kitchen's shining white linoleum. "I heard a lot of threats while I was on the force. It taught me a thing or two, y'know?" He began counting on his fingers: "Some very peculiar things have been going on at Twin Acres. You're getting weird phone calls, midnight visitors who aren't there, tire slashings, a note with a message very much like mine, yet you can't add two and two."

Elice matched his defiant stare. "I did very well in math, thank you, despite being a girl, and I feel I must point out that you're mixing your variables. What appears to be two and two may very well be nothing of the kind."

The argument was pointless. And nothing annoyed Cabot

more than useless conversation. "I love you! I want you safe and happy. Can't you get that through your thick head?" It was neither the time nor the place for such a proclamation, yet Cabot felt relieved to have finally spoken the truth.

She tried to hide her grin behind a stern frown. "Oh, stop looking so red-faced," she said. "I never said I didn't understand your motives." She hugged him tightly and looked up into his face. "But that doesn't mean you're right. And, by the way," she added, "I love you, too."

Cabot met her eyes. "You will put new locks on the doors. On the windows, too."

"I won't."

"It's either that, or we'll just have to get married right away, so I can keep an eye on you twenty-four hours a day."

She tucked in one corner of her mouth. "Don't you threaten me, Cabot Murray." Standing on tiptoe, she planted a quick kiss on his chin. "I hope you've learned something here this morning."

For as long as he'd known her, she'd never been one to keep her opinions to herself. Cabot waited, knowing she'd soon explain herself. He didn't have to wait long.

"Next time you have an attack of Swollen Ego," she said with a smile and a wink, "I want you to remember that the world revolves around no one. Not even someone who kisses as great as you do."

He was about to respond to her blatant invitation when Annie ran into the room. "Mommy, Grandma is on the phone."

"I never even heard the phone ring," he said, stunned.

"I unplugged the one in here so I could paint over the jack," she explained, connecting the wires so that she could talk to her mother-in-law.

"Mrs. Glasser," she said, "how are you?"

"I'm fine, honey. Tried to call last night, but nobody answered. Marge told me you'd be at Foggy Bottom today. Gave me the number. I hear you're helping Cabot redecorate. How nice . . . ."

Why did she feel guilty? She wasn't married to Mrs. Glasser's son any longer. "We. . .uh. . . ." Elice didn't know what to tell Bobby's mother. "We were out."

Mrs. Glasser laughed. "So Annie said."

Elice hid her face behind her free hand. If Annie had filled Mrs. Glasser in, there was no telling what the woman had heard.

"She adores him, Elice," her mother-in-law was saying. "He sounds too good to be true." Snickering, she added, "Tall, handsome, funny. . . . Why have you been keeping him a secret?"

"I'm not. It's just. . . . I've been awfully busy. . . ."

"You'd better grab him before somebody else does, honey. I've seen him in town." Mrs. Glasser whistled. "If I weren't a happily married woman, I'd snap him up myself."

Elice stared into the earpiece, thinking she'd either gone crazy or had a bad connection. Had Bobby's mother actually said that?

"You know, Bob and I were beginning to worry about you, Elice. You spend entirely too much time alone with those kids. It's not healthy. . .for them or for you. You need some adult companionship. Of the male variety, I might add. Which reminds me. From what Annie says, you and that wonderful man never spend any time alone. Tell me it isn't true."

"Well, it's a little hard to find sitters and—"

"Don't you say another word, Elice. I know Bob and I are getting up in years, but those grandchildren of ours are about the best-behaved kids in the state. I think we can handle them for a couple of hours now and then. Having children under foot all the time isn't my idea of romantic."

Romantic? Elice shook her head. She must have inhaled too many paint fumes.

"I'll tell you what, honey. It's been a long time since Bob and I have taken the kids anywhere. We were planning a trip to Ocean City for the week. Won't you let them come with us? We'll come pick them up this evening."

Elice chewed her lower lip. That would certainly solve a lot of problems. For one, the kids would be out of the house. She couldn't believe the melodramatic thought that followed: Out of danger. "I don't suppose Annie mentioned his name, did she?"

"Didn't have to. Every woman in Freeland is whispering about him. It isn't every day a man that handsome rides into town, you know." When Mrs. Glasser laughed like that, it was hard to believe she was in her late sixties. "I can't wait to meet him, though," she added. "What time would you like Bob and I to meet you at your place?"

Elice glanced at her watch. "In an hour or so?"

"It's time you put Bobby behind you. He was my only son, but God knows you deserved better. If being with Cabot makes you happy, Bob and I are all for it."

He was standing there, grinning at her when she hung up. "I take it the in-laws approve of me?"

She pshawed him. "That's only because they don't know you the way I do."

"But they're taking the kids away for a week?"

She ignored his mischievous wink. "I have to get home and pack their things."

He nodded, his grin gone now. "Couldn't have asked for better timing."

"I told you the Lord would take care of things."

He rolled his eyes. "If He was so good at taking care of things, there wouldn't be so many things to take care of, now would there?"

She hated it when he talked that way. Elice had been praying, ever since the relationship began to look like it might become more than a friendship, that the Lord would show Cabot the way back to Him. So far, it didn't look like that was happening. And if he didn't start exhibiting some signs of Christianity soon, she was going to be faced with some very difficult decisions, because Elice had vowed at Bobby's graveside never to involve herself with a non-believer again.

Example. That's what he needs, she decided. She'd just have to set such a good example that he'd have no choice but to see that her way. . .God's way. . .was the only way. She grinned. "Don't get me started," she warned, wagging her forefinger under his nose. "Don't even think about getting me started."

four

Elice had just washed the last dish when the phone rang.

"Hi, pretty lady," Cabot said.

She considered saying, "Hi, Mr. Wonderful." "Hi, yourself," she said instead.

"Wally wears black-soled work boots, doesn't he?"

Frowning, Elice said, "I never really paid much attention to the bottoms of his shoes. What a strange question."

Cabot chuckled. "Not when you consider that the scuff mark on your counter was put there by a black-soled boot."

She sighed. "Cabot," she said, her voice a warning, "I told you, Walter didn't have anything to do with what happened here the—"

"You're wearing out my patience. There are footprints under your kitchen window, size twelves. I checked. Wally wears size twelve. The impressions have cleats in them . . .his boots have cleats."

"Well, if you know so much, why bother asking me what kind of shoes he wears!" she snapped. Elice ran a trembling hand through her hair. Walter? Under the kitchen window? She couldn't make herself believe he'd been there at all, let alone believe he could have been responsible for the frightening things that had been happening at Twin Acres lately.

It was Cabot's turn to sigh. "I only called to tell you I might be a little late picking you up for dinner, because I'm going to pay Wally a little visit."

"You're actually going to grill that poor man simply

because he wears work boots. . .like almost every man in Freeland?"

"I'm not going to grill him because of his shoes," he said, impatience tingeing his voice. "I'm not going to 'grill' him at all." Cabot sighed again. "Someone broke into your house and, without more evidence, the police can't find out who it was. I'm going to get it for them so they can make an arrest that'll stick."

"This is ridiculous."

"You're ridiculous!" The moment the words were out of his mouth, he regretted them.

"Walter isn't your bad guy, Cabot. I'll bet he doesn't even know how to type. Besides, he adores you, so that blows your 'get even with Cabot' theory right out of the water."

He recalled the argument they'd had last night after they'd left his house to pack the kids' suitcases. The two of them had greeted Mr. and Mrs. Glasser, gave the ocean-bound party hearty goodbye hugs, and warned them not to get too much sun. The house had seemed so quiet and empty after they had left that he'd suggested a drive to Shrewsbury. But not even her favorite—soft ice cream with chocolate sprinkles—brightened Elice's mood. "Stop looking so glum," he'd teased; "they'll only be gone a week." And she'd said, "If I look glum, it's your fault, not the kids', because you've turned your back on God."

The argument had lasted less than a minute, but the stony silence had hung in the air all night. When he'd tried to kiss her goodbye, she offered her cheek. "I love you more than I ever dreamed I could love any man," she'd said softly, "but I love the Lord more. I want to share everything with you, and that includes my faith. If I can't. . . ."

He'd taken her in his arms then, and explained that old habits die hard; he'd only behaved badly because he felt responsible that his past had put her in danger. As he saw it, Wally was the prime suspect in his "get Cabot" theory. "If you had even a glimmer of faith living inside of you," she'd scolded, "you couldn't say that. You wouldn't even be able to think it."

She'd been praying about it, quite a lot, she'd told him; if Wally had had anything to do with the scary stuff that had been occurring at Foggy Bottom and Twin Acres, she'd know because, as she put it, "The Lord would have shown me the truth."

"Well, what do you have to say about that?" Elice asked.

He'd been so lost in the remembrance of it all that he'd forgotten Elice was on the phone.

"What do I have to say about what?"

"About your 'get Cabot' theory."

"I don't have any answers, Elice. Just a lot of questions."

"Stupid questions, if you ask me."

"Well, I didn't ask you." He didn't know how much more of this righteous indignation he could stand. He'd always been a law-abiding citizen. He paid his taxes, in full and on time, donated a hefty chunk of change to various charities every year, tried to do unto others, and all that. Who did she think she was, anyway, to insinuate he wasn't good enough for her, simply because he didn't believe in God in the same way she did?

"I wish you wouldn't go to Walter's. You'll confuse him. At the very least, you'll hurt his feelings if you tell him what you suspect."

"So now you're an expert in psychology and police work."

She cleared her throat, then said, "You needn't concern yourself with being late, Cabot. I'd rather spend the evening alone. I have a lot of thinking to do."

She didn't want to see him, and that broke his heart. But

he was angry, too. No one had ever judged him before. He believed she was doing exactly that. And he didn't like it. Not one bit. "You mean praying, don't you?" His voice dripped with sarcasm. "You going to ask God if He approves of me?"

Silence.

"Well? Are you?"

"Yes, I'm going to pray about you. But mostly, I'm going to pray for you."

He laughed. "I don't need your prayers, Elice. Besides, what makes you think the Big Guy would go to bat for me? He's never done it before. I know, because I've asked. On my feet, on my hands and knees, flat on my face. . . ."

"You're so lost, you're not even aware of it."

One. . .five. . .ten seconds ticked by before he said, "I'm sorry if I offended you. I wouldn't hurt you for the world. You know that, don't you?"

She hesitated a moment, then said, "I know you wouldn't consciously hurt me."

"But I'm not a Bible-reading, church-going, blind follower, like you, so I'm hurting you subconsciously, right?"

"You're hurting yourself far more than you're hurting me. If only you'd—"

"Elice, can't we just agree to disagree on this subject?" he interrupted. "I miss you. I want to see that gorgeous face of yours and spend an entire, uninterrupted evening alone with you."

She hesitated before saying, "I don't think it's a very good idea to—"

That does it! he decided. "All right, then," he said, with all the patience he could muster. "Maybe you're right. Maybe it's best we stop seeing each other, for everybody's sake."

He heard her sharp intake of air.

"But I want you to know that I'm here for you, if you ever need me." Cabot wanted her to say she couldn't live without him, hoped she'd ask him to hurry right over, because she missed him, too, and was waiting for an invitation to spend a quiet evening eating popcorn and watching old black-and-white movies on TV. But, after a full minute of silence, he quietly hung up.

Cabot sat in his easy chair and stared at the phone for a long time. He'd tried everything else, and in his moment of desperation, he tried it her way: "Lord," he prayed aloud, "make her call. Please, let her call."

He waited. Five minutes passed, then ten. An hour later, he was still staring at the soundless phone. The longer he stared at it, the harder it got to swallow the sob aching in his throat. "You big jerk," he said aloud, swiping angrily at his tears, "see what you get for not sticking to your motto?"

Cabot gave the still silent phone one last sad glance. Then he got to his feet. He'd talk to Wally, no matter what she said. He'd poke around and dig around and search until he dug up the evidence the police needed to put away the nut who was harassing her. "At least she'll have the good deed to remember you by," he said under his breath, slamming the kitchen door behind him.

&

It didn't matter whether or not he'd done the right thing in ending their relationship. Cabot missed her terribly, missed those kids, too. Eventually, he knew, he'd adjust to their absence. But, like getting used to life without Maggie and Lindy, it would take time, a whole lot of it.

And he spent most of that time on the farm. Foggy Bottom was finally beginning to look like the place where he'd grown up. Orderly precision, from the fences to the barn doors, made it clear to anyone who passed by that someone cared about the place again.

When he wasn't digging or painting or hammering, Cabot was out hunting down clues. One by one, he flipped through the snapshots he'd taken that day of the area around Elice's kitchen window, comparing the black streak on her counter to the one he'd found on Wally's kitchen floor.

Wally had a beat-up portable typewriter, and Cabot rolled a sheet of paper into it and used his forefingers to type "Every good boy does fine." As he'd expected, each *e* tilted slightly to the left, just like the ones in the ominous notes he and Elice had received. And a stack of that same blue paper sat on the table beside the typewriter.

Cabot liked Wally. He hadn't wanted to believe the big guy had been involved in any way with the goings-on at Foggy Bottom and Twin Acres. But every shred of evidence incriminated the slow-witted ex-soldier.

"Where'd you get this old thing?" Cabot asked him.

Wally scratched his head. "Found it in the shed. Mr. Olson said if I cleaned it up and bought a new ribbon, I could have it."

Cabot struck the *e* key again, a small part of him hoping that by some small miracle, it would stand up straight this time. "This is where you keep the typewriter? All the time?"

Wally nodded. " 'Cept for when Mr. Jack borrows it."

He'd been staring at the sentence he'd typed, but at Wally's statement, Cabot's hazel eyes fused to the man's blue ones. "Except for when Jack borrows it?" he repeated.

Wally's blond brows rose. "He don't have a typewriter," Wally explained, "so he borrows mine to write letters to the editor." Smiling, he added, "Did you see the one he wrote in yesterday's paper? About truck drivers speeding up and down New Freedom Road?"

Cabot frowned. "No. I'm afraid I missed it."

"I got it right here," he said. "Want to read it?"

He shook his head. "Thanks anyway; maybe I'll look it up when I get home." Cabot stared hard at Wally. He'd learned to depend on his gut instinct. It had saved his life, and the lives of a partner or two, while working Chicago's streets. Right now, that instinct was telling him that Wally couldn't do a mean thing if his life depended on it. Still, maybe he knew something that would point Cabot in the right direction.

He sat across from him at the table and took a sip of the iced cola Wally had poured for him when he'd arrived. "When was the first time Jack borrowed your typewriter?"

Wally squinted. " 'Bout two months ago, I spoze."

Cabot nodded and absently drew a smiley face in the condensation that had formed on his glass. "How many times has he used it?"

" 'Bout three times, I guess."

"Only three?"

Wally nodded. "Kept it about a week each time. Gave me five bucks when he brought it back, too," he added, grinning. "I used the money for cage supplies. For my pets. Say! Do you want to see my pets?"

Cabot chuckled. "Why not?"

It took a full half-hour for Wally to introduce Cabot to each insect, describe its species and diet, and detail the building of its cage. Cabot found it difficult to pay attention. He was too busy thinking about Jack; about how he'd borrowed Wally's typewriter at almost exactly the same times the blue notes were delivered to Foggy Bottom and Twin Acres. Coincidence? Cabot didn't think so.

As Wally rambled on about his so-called pets, Cabot complimented his attention to detail. "You could probably make a lot of money building dollhouse furniture," he admitted, "as good as you are at building things on a small scale. There are thousands of dollhouse enthusiasts who buy tiny furniture. You could advertise in antiques magazines."

Wally's grin nearly split his face in two. "You really think so? That's a great idea! Will you help me get started?"

Cabot patted his new buddy's back. "Sure. Sure." He sat at the table again and finished his soda. "Tell me something, Wally."

Wally met his eyes.

"How do you feel about Elice?"

Immediately, his cheeks flushed and he stared at his hands folded quietly in his lap. "She's way too pretty and way too smart for somebody like me." He looked back at Cabot. "Besides," he said, grinning crookedly, "she's in love with you."

Cabot shifted uncomfortably in his chair, remembering their last conversation. "I'm not so sure about that."

Wally nodded. "I am. She said so. I heard her myself."

Leaning forward, he asked, "She did? When?"

The ruddy cheeks reddened again. "When I was. . . ." His eyes darted from his fingertips to Cabot's face and back again. "She's got a voice like an angel. Did you know that?"

Cabot smiled.

"She sings while she washes dishes and sometimes when she's making supper. Makes me feel good inside, hearing her pretty voice."

"You heard her from your hiding place under her window?"

Wally's eyes widened. "How did you know?"

Cabot shrugged. "I was a cop, remember?"

Fear widened Wally's eyes even more. "You won't tell her, will you? If she ever found out, she might think I'm weird or something, and quit being my friend."

Cabot stopped smiling. "I won't tell her. But you're going to stop hiding in her bushes. It's against the law, you know."

The blond brows rose again. "Honest? I promise, Cabot. I'll never do it again."

He leaned both elbows on the table. "Good. Now, I have something to tell you, Wally, and it's got to stay between you and me. If you repeat this to anyone, Elice's life could be in danger. Will you help me protect her?"

The brows nearly met in the center of Wally's forehead. "Protect her from what?"

It took all of fifteen minutes to fill Wally in on what had been going on at Foggy Bottom and Twin Acres. Cabot didn't leave out a single detail. He discovered that if he spoke slowly, and enunciated well, Wally comprehended everything he said. When he was finished, Cabot held out his hand. "So we have a deal? You'll help me protect Elice and the kids?"

Wally stared at Cabot's big hand, then pumped his arm up and down. "Anything you say, Cabot." He paused, still squeezing the ex-cop's hand. "Say. . .are we friends now?"

Cabot placed his free hand on Wally's shoulder and grinned. "You bet we are."

❧

It was hard to believe that so many days had passed. It had taken every ounce of strength that Elice could muster to keep from picking up the phone and dialing his number. But she'd made the right decision. She was sure of it. As long as she continued to pray hard and long, she'd be able to stick to it.

On the morning the Glassers were to return home from the beach, they called to say they'd booked their condo for an additional week. Elice wanted to protest. "Bring them home right this minute!" she wanted to say, "because I miss them desperately." But Mrs. Glasser put the children on the phone, one at a time, and the joy in their voices was so apparent that she couldn't bear to deny them another week of fun in the sun.

Still, without the children around, Elice had too much time on her hands. With no one to cook for or clean up after, she found herself wandering aimlessly around the house, search- ing for something to do. She'd completed every sign ahead of schedule and had even finished several that weren't due for weeks. The house sparkled from top to bottom. And a weed didn't dare show itself in the vegetable or flower gar- dens, for fear she'd be there to snatch it from the ground the moment she got a glimpse of green.

She baked bread, put up thirty quarts of green beans and tomatoes, and made a dozen peach pies and froze them. But, regardless of how busy she kept herself, her mind refused to focus on the task at hand. It seemed to want to think of one thing, and one thing only—Cabot.

She missed his laughing eyes, his merry chuckle, the way he could turn the most mundane moment into a rip-roaring good time. He'd taught Danny to string a fishing line, showed Annie how to tie her sneakers, helped Emily learn to use the computerized card catalog at the library, and had made Elice realize she didn't want to live out the rest of her life alone, after all.

She'd grown accustomed to seeing his big work boots beside the back door, his denim jacket on the hall tree, his broad-shouldered body in her easy chair. She'd gotten used to having him help with the supper dishes, wearing her frilly white apron, his sleeves rolled up to the elbow. She'd even grown to like the way he stacked spoons in the silverware drawer, one on top of the other. She'd even started to think of his phone calls first thing in the morning and last thing every night as part of her daily routine. No amount of hard work could erase the loneliness from her heart. Not even prayer dulled the nonstop ache of his absence.

In six days, she told herself, the kids would be home. God created the entire universe in that amount of time; certainly she could manage to get along—alone—for just six more days. She'd gotten used to life without Bobby in time, and she'd get used to being without Cabot, too. You just have to keep reminding yourself he's not a believer, she told herself, and the Lord will help you get through this thing.

Elice's inner turmoil became almost too predictable: *He's not a believer, but his patience and sensitivity reminds me of Jesus'.*

He says he's angry with God, but he says just what the children need to hear, precisely when they need to hear it.

He refuses to admit he needs the Lord in his life, but he has no problem admitting how much he wants you in it.

The Lord will get you through this, she told herself again, and again, and again.

❧

Cabot hadn't had the dream in ages. But the night of their breakup, it came back, like an unwelcome ghost, to haunt him. To Cabot, it was a lot like fast-forwarding and rewinding the scariest part of a horror movie:

He'd heard the call on his police radio, and recognized the dispatcher's staccato listing of license plate numbers. He was both thankful and surprised that his car could actually go the hundred and twenty miles an hour promised by the speedometer as he sped from the station to the accident

.scene. "Please, God," he prayed as he raced through the streets, "let it be a mistake. Don't let it be Maggie and Lindy."

Two fire trucks, three ambulances, and dozens of squad cars blocked his path, and Cabot had been forced to park nearly a block away. He ran the entire distance full-out, and when he broke through the crowd of curious onlookers, he saw Maggie's little red sedan, engulfed in flames. He heard them, calling his name. He saw them, trying to reach for him from behind the smoke-filled windows. Cabot tried to shoulder his way to the front of the crowd. Several officers grabbed him. "Hey, buddy; you can't go in there," they shouted. "You'll be killed!" He fought them off. "That's my family in there," he screamed. "If I don't go in, they'll be killed!"

A surge of superhuman strength enabled Cabot to free himself from the officers' hold, and he ran up to the car. The only thing that separated him from Maggie and Lindy now was the window. "Can you roll it down?" he shouted at Maggie.

"Stuck," she said, coughing, her sooty hands gripping her throat; her terrified eyes fused to his.

"Dear Lord," he prayed, grabbing the door handle, "help me. Give me the strength to get them out of there." Instinct made him snatch back his hand as the hot metal scorched his palm. He yanked off his suitcoat, planning to use it as a hotpad. "Okay, Lord," he prayed aloud, "it's just You and me now. We're all they've got—"

And then the car exploded.

The huge fireball propelled Cabot backward, rendering him unconscious. When he woke in the hospital, he saw his partner asleep in the chair beside his bed. Cabot ached all over, but his head hurt worst of all. Glancing around carefully, he saw his right arm in a sling, his left hand bandaged. But nothing made sense. Why was he here? Had he been wounded on the job?

"Hey," he whispered, nudging Clancy awake. "Hey, Joe."

The red-haired man came to and sat up.

"I'm gonna report this to the captain," Cabot whispered, grinning as much as his swollen, bruised jaw would allow. "Napping on the job is against regulations."

Clancy didn't smile back. And since Clancy was always smiling, it scared Cabot. "What's going on, Joe? Why am I here?"

"There was an accident," his partner said softly. "On the Dan Ryan Expressway. . . ."

It came back in an agonizing flash that was almost as blinding as the fire itself: Red car. Red flames. Maggie's red hair. Lindy's little red lips screaming his name. . . .

Cabot sat up, grimacing with pain. "Where are they?" he asked, swinging his legs over the side of the bed. "In pediatrics? In the emergency room?" He grabbed the front of Clancy's shirt, oblivious to the pain of his burned palm. "Where are they! Tell me where they are, before I deck you!"

Clancy gently shoved him back onto the mattress. "They're gone, Cabot."

He blinked up at his partner. "Gone? You mean to Shock Trauma? Well, go get the car. They'll need me. What are you waiting for!"

Clancy only shook his head sadly and repeated, "Cabot, listen to me. Maggie and Lindy are gone."

Gone? he thought. *As in* dead*? But how could that be? I prayed like a crazy man all the way from the station to the accident. Every word out of my mouth was aimed right straight at God's ear. Surely He didn't let them. . . .*

"What do you mean. . .they're gone?"

Clancy sighed heavily. "Why me?" he asked the ceiling. "I mean gone, Cabot. G-o-n-e. Please don't make me say it. . . ."

A deep furrow formed on his brow as he tried to fight back the tears. "You're lying. He wouldn't do this to us. To me. All my life, I've believed. He wouldn't do this. He couldn't do this. . . ."

"Who?" Clancy wanted to know. "Who wouldn't do what?"

He lay back against the cool, crisp pillowcase and covered his face with his hands. Nurses, doctors, paramedics—everyone in the E.R.—looked over at him when the mournful wailing began. Then, as though embarrassed to have intruded on his grief, each looked away, and pretended to be engrossed in his work.

It stopped there every time, and just as surely as "The End" showed up at the conclusion of every movie, Cabot woke from the dream, groggy and perspiring, his heart beating fast, tears streaming down his face.

He'd had the dream every night since the breakup with Elice. He believed it was a symbol of sorts. A symbol that proved she was out of his life, just as surely as Maggie and Lindy were out of it, for good.

He'd tried to stave off the horrible nightmare, but nothing worked. Not long days filled with hard work. Not reading until dawn. Not even several days without sleep at all.

Nothing ventured, nothing lost, he reminded himself. *You'd be beyond all this now if you'd only listened to your own good advice.*

The phone rang, and he lay down the hatchet he'd been absently grazing across the pumice stone on the kitchen table.

"Why are you mad at us?"

"Annie? Hey, there! I didn't know you were back. Did you have a good time at the ocean?"

"Yes," she said tentatively. "But why are you mad at us?"

He licked his lips. "I'm not mad at you, Annie. Whatever gave you that idea?"

"You never call. You never come over anymore. And Mommy cries a lot. Every night. She doesn't think we know, but we can hear her in there."

Cabot ran a hand through his hair. "Well, darlin', it's sort of like this. While you guys were on vacation, your mommy and I had an argument."

"What about?"

And what did he say to that?

She started to cry. "Don't you love us anymore?"

His heart ached. He was about to tell her he loved her. That he loved Danny, and Emily, and her mommy, too—especially her mommy—when Annie hung up. He hadn't felt so helpless or useless since the funerals. Trembling, Cabot picked up the hatchet and ran the blade along the pumice stone again. The phone rang again, startling him so badly, he cut his thumb on the hatchet's sharp edge. "Ouch!" he whispered, and instinctively stuck the thumb into his mouth.

"Cabot, I want to know what's going on."

"Emily," he said around his thumb.

"Are you and Mom. . .?" The girl hesitated, as if searching for the right word.

Emily, at nearly eleven, was wise beyond her years. Elice had told him that tests at school showed her to be at least five years ahead of her peers, academically. He realized early on in their relationship that she was at least that far ahead emotionally, too.

"Was it a fight over something stupid, or is this permanent?"

He wanted to slam the phone down, fire up the Jeep, and storm into Elice's house, demanding a reconciliation. But he hadn't found out enough about their mystery visitor yet and, until he did, his presence was a danger to them. Besides, he still hadn't become a blind follower of her God, so such a visit would be pointless.

"It wasn't a fight, Emi," he said. "I prefer to call it a disagreement."

He listened to her long, quiet pause.

"So you're saying you don't love Mom anymore?"

"Of course not!" he said instantly. "I'd never say that!" What was that he heard—giggling?

"I'll call you later, Cabot," she said, and hung up.

Cabot stared at the phone for a moment before hanging up himself, a confused frown etched on his handsome face. "Now, what do you suppose that was all about?" he asked aloud, wrapping his bleeding thumb in a paper napkin.

❧

"We've got to do something. They're too stubborn to fix this all by themselves," Danny said.

"Maybe Grandmom can help," Annie suggested.

"I already talked to Grandmom," Emily said. "She says she'll talk it over with Granddad and get back to us. But grownups talk things to death. We don't have time for that. We have to do something now."

"So, what are we waitin' for?" Danny asked, sitting cross-legged on his bedroom floor. His sisters joined him. Several minutes passed as the children sat in their tiny circle, frowning with concentration. Then, suddenly, Emily's face lit up.

"I've got it!" she said, waving her siblings closer.

The three huddled close, whispering and giggling.

❧

"Now, who can that be so early in the morning?" Elice wondered aloud as she opened the front door.

"Hi, Missus Glasser." Jimmy, Marge King's oldest son, stood on the porch with an armful of red roses. "These are for you."

"What on earth. . .?" Elice stared at the huge bouquet for a moment, then said, "Danny, bring me my purse, please?"

Elice put the big blue glass vase on the coffee table, pulled a dollar from her wallet, and handed it to Jimmy. "Thanks," she told him. "Tell your mom I said hello."

"Sure will, Missus Glasser," he said as she closed the door.

"It isn't my birthday," she said mostly to herself as she reached for the tiny envelope.

Emily grabbed Danny and Annie by their shirt collars and dragged them into her bedroom. "We can't go in there. She'll see through us like window glass. Follow me!"

They thundered toward the back door. "We're going to ride our bikes over to the Becks', Mom," Emily called from the porch. "I'm wearing my watch, so we'll be home by five. I promise."

She'd just unsheathed the card. "Okay," she said distractedly as she read the neat script created by one of Mr. Thompson's florists:

> *To my pretty lady,*
> *I miss you. I love you. I'm sorry.*
> *Cabot*

Elice bit her lower lip and held the card against her chest. Tears welled in her eyes. *Could this mean there's a chance for us, after all?* she wondered. She reread the card. *Could it mean he found his way back to the Lord in the weeks we've been apart?*

Kneeling beside the coffee table, she cupped one velvety blossom in her palm and closed her eyes as she inhaled its fragrance. Nothing had ever smelled sweeter. Sitting back on her heels, Elice touched the delicate buds. Ran her fingertip along a smooth green leaf. Smiling, her heart swelled with warmth and love for the gentle giant who'd been responsible for the delivery of this precious and romantic gift.

Suddenly, the doorbell rang, interrupting the touching moment. This time, Billy Beck stood on the porch, holding a long rectangular box. "These are for you, Missus Glasser," he said, poking the huge red satin bow.

She fished another dollar bill from her wallet and exchanged it for the white box. "Thanks, Billy."

"Mom said to tell you she'd see you in church on Sunday," he said as he climbed back into the truck. She watched the white panel van that had WILHIDE's in big green letters on its side, back down her driveway, then turned her attention to the card that read:

> *To the woman of my dreams*
> *With my heartfelt apologies and all of my love.*
> *Cabot*

She took a deep breath and lifted the lid. Inside, twelve white roses nestled on a bed of green tissue paper, surrounded by feathery ferns and delicate baby's breath. Taking one rose from its resting place, she held it beneath her nose and inhaled deeply. A little giggle popped from her lips. "Two dozen roses, and there's no special occasion!"

No one had ever sent her roses before. *Leave it to Cabot to be the first,* she thought, flushing like a schoolgirl in the throes of a full-blown crush. *As soon as I put these into water,* she told herself, giggling, *I'm going to give that man a piece of my mind!*

❧

The five of them leaned against Mr. Glasser's big black Cadillac. "You're kidding!" Mrs. Glasser giggled. "But where'd you get the money!"

"It was left over from what you and Granddad gave us at the ocean," Emily explained.

The grandmother laughed. "Do you believe it, Bob? Seems these kids have a lot of their grandfather's blood coursing in their veins!"

Grinning, her husband nodded. "Great minds think alike, I always say."

"Elice is probably dizzy with glee by now," she said, smiling.

"Do you think it'll work?" Danny asked.

"It had better work," said his grandfather, "or the bunch of us just spent seventy-five dollars for nothing!"

"And just wait till Cabot gets a load of what we delivered to Foggy Bottom. . .with your mama's name on it," Mrs. Glasser added.

"Two loaves of honey bread and an apple pie," Mr. Glasser said.

"If you kids hadn't told us they were his favorites, I'd never have known what to bake."

Emily snickered. "I'm scared to go home."

Danny joined her. "Me, too. Will you come with us, guys?"

The grandparents hugged. "I have a better idea," Mrs. Glasser said. "How 'bout you kids spend the night at our house. That way, when they get around to thanking each other for the lovely gifts, they can kiss and make up in private."

All five of them laughed heartily.

They were very pleased with their little matchmaking scheme.

❧

As she dialed his number, her heart raced. How long had it been since she'd heard his wonderful voice? Had it really been nearly three weeks? *Lord,* she prayed, smiling happily, *guide my words. Please don't let me gush too badly.*

After the tenth ring, she hung up, disappointment and a certain sadness registering in her heart. They'd wasted enough time over the silly argument. She didn't want to lose another precious moment.

Elice jumped into the car and headed for Foggy Bottom. Halfway there, she saw him, headed in the opposite direction. They stopped, right there in the middle of New Freedom Road, grinning like a couple of love-starved fools.

"I was just on my way over to your place."

"And I was just on my way to see you," she said.

"I wanted to thank you. Everything was delicious."

She'd imagined it would be wonderful to hear his voice again, to see his handsome face again, but Elice hadn't counted on feeling quite so giddy. She must be hearing things. "Delicious?"

"The bread, of course. And that pie." He smacked his lips. "But I didn't enjoy either nearly as much as this note of yours." Cabot paused. "I didn't know you even had a typewriter."

Elice frowned. "I don't." Then, "What bread?" And after a moment, "What pie?"

His brows furrowed slightly. "When I got back from town

a few minutes ago, I found them in a basket on my front porch, wrapped in a red-and-white tablecloth. I followed instructions to the letter." He reached across the front seat and grabbed a sheet of rumpled paper. "'Have a slice of each immediately,'" he quoted, " 'because they're symbols of how much I've missed your sweetness and—' "

"I think I smell a rat," she interrupted, narrowing her eyes.

"Anything but, pretty lady. That stuff smelled heavenly."

"Cabot," she interrupted gently, "did you send me roses?"

He laughed. "Roses?"

"A dozen white ones and a dozen red ones?"

"You told me once that you hated cut flowers because cutting them was a waste of their beauty. You said if a man ever sent you roses in a box, you'd box his ears." His left brow rose high on his forehead. "Wait a minute. Who's sending you roses if I'm not?"

A horn tooted behind him.

"We're blocking traffic," he said. "Meet me at the little park up ahead. Seems we have a lot to discuss."

Nodding, she shifted into drive and headed for the children's playground the Chamber of Commerce had constructed last summer. That's when she remembered the silly-yet-guilty expressions on the faces of her children, who'd skedaddled from the house awfully quickly, now that she thought about it.

He parked beside her and they exited their vehicles simultaneously.

"You were right," she admitted, smiling. "I don't smell a rat. . .I smell three."

He took her in his arms and held her close.

"The kids, huh?"

Elice nodded against his chest. "Um-hmm."

He held her closer. "Feels good to have you back where

you belong. I've missed you."

"Feels good to be here. I've missed you, too."

"Then all's forgiven?"

"And forgotten."

"Thank God."

She met his eyes. "Does that mean what I think it means?"

He grinned. "Let's just say you made me realize I have to at least give God a chance."

She hugged him tighter. "Goes to show you, He answers prayers."

His eyes widened. "You mean you've been praying I'd come back?"

"Every morning and every night and every spare minute in between."

Cabot rested his chin on the top of her head. "You say the roses came by way of the florist?"

"How else?"

"Hmmm." He leaned back and looked into her face. "So how'd they get the goodies over to my house? It's too far to go by bicycle."

"Hmmm," she echoed. "It's beginning to look like we're overrun by rats, and some of them drive black Cadillacs."

Cabot dropped a gentle kiss on her lips. "Funny," he said, "but I've suddenly developed a great fondness for the fuzzy little beasts."

five

The bed was much too short for Cabot's frame, but it didn't
matter. He didn't think he'd sleep much anyway. He clicked
on the lamp beside Danny's bed and lay upon the colorful
sportscar bedspread, then folded his hands under his head
and glanced at the trucks and cars atop the dresser, then at
the posters of Air Force jets that hung on every wall. He
listened to the electric hum of the alarm on the nightstand.
Three o'clock, glowed the dial. Cabot wondered if, down
the hall in her own room, Elice thought of him, too.

Cabot sat up with a start. *What was that?* he wondered.
Footsteps? Immediately, he turned out the light.

There it was again. Yes. . .footsteps—definitely.

The kids were safe at the Glassers' house, he'd told her;
it's the perfect opportunity to catch whoever is pulling these
ridiculous, albeit dangerous, stunts. It had taken nearly half
an hour to convince her to let him stay. "The neighbors
won't know that you're asleep in Danny's bed," she gasped.
"They'll think. . . ." She'd blushed so deeply that he'd taken
her in his arms so she couldn't see his grin, and promised to
park the Jeep behind the shed out back so the neighbors
wouldn't know he was there at all.

He slipped silently out of the bed and into his shoes, glad
he hadn't yet removed his pants and shirt, then tiptoed
through the quiet hall and into the living room. *Someone's
out there, all right,* he told himself, *and not a small someone, either.* The silhouette looked strangely familiar, and
then he remembered the shadow in his pines.

90

She'd taken his advice, and changed the locks. He tried to remember where she'd put the key that unlocked the double-deadbolt. Once he'd found it, hanging on a tiny nail beside the door jamb, he cautiously stuck it into the lock and turned slowly, wincing when it clicked into the open position and shattered the silence of the night.

His palm was sweating, and when he grabbed the brass knob, it made opening the door impossible. Cabot dried his hand on the seat of his pants, then tried again. He'd thought about oiling that squeak in the hinges several times. Now, as the high-pitched squeal grated in his ears, he wished he'd done it.

Finally, the door was open far enough for him to slip onto the porch. He stood there for a long moment, studying the blackened yard for a sign of that shadow. In the dim light of the moon, he could see the tree swing, swaying slowly in the breeze. Beside it, a red plastic sand bucket rolled lazily left, then right. Annie's tricycle caught a moonbeam and reflected it onto the fender of Danny's dirt bike, leaning on the shed wall. The toys reminded him that three innocent children lived in this house.

Something moved near the clothesline, and his eyes riveted to the spot. Crouching, he made his way into the yard and focused on the thing he'd seen. Then he watched it move steadily closer to the north side of Elice's house, then disappear into the inky darkness.

There were three windows over there: one in Danny's room and two in Elice's. He was on the lawn now, nearly running to keep up with the quickening pace of the shadow and being careful to stay behind shrubs and tree trunks. A bead of sweat stung his eye, and Cabot swiped it away.

Black leather-gloved hands rested on the window sill. One booted foot balanced on the brick garden wall below it. One good push, Cabot realized, and the shadow would be inside. . .in her room. Only the screen separated her from this maniac. He had no choice. If he didn't grab the shadow now, Cabot may not get another chance. He darted forward and lunged at it.

Pain shot through his side. Looking up, he saw the gleaming, curved blade of a hunting knife. As darkness had been his partner up until now, the moon's glow was now his nightlight, and he saw the near-black blood that covered the blade.

Rolling over, he managed to escape further injury. But his wound was more than superficial. He'd been hurt enough times in Chicago to know that much. He'd have to act quickly, before he passed out from loss of blood or shock or both. Before the shadow realized how badly he'd hurt Cabot, it took advantage of his position and made its way into Elice's window.

Did the shadow plan to stab her, too? Had it come here tonight intending to. . .kill?

Cabot did the only thing he could think to do, and threw his weight against the shadow, knocking it off balance. Knocking the weapon from its hand, too. But the would-be intruder was up again, immediately. On its feet and running. Cabot reached for the ski mask, and tried to tear it from the intruder's head. He wanted more than anything, right now, to see who had been responsible for this whole unbelievable mess.

But Cabot's strength was waning. Dizziness crept up, slowly and without warning. He steadied himself against the trunk of a maple tree and breathed raggedly as he watched the shadow scurry, like a cornered rat, along the hedgerow that lined Elice's property, across the road, and out of sight. But not before blasting Cabot's temple with a well-placed blow from his elbow.

Holding his side and head alternately, Cabot limped toward the back porch. Elice, standing there in the doorway, nearly scared him out of his wits. "I heard the noise," she whispered, "and then you screamed."

"Screamed? Who, me? I don't remember screaming," he said, holding the porch rail for support. And then, like a puppet whose puppeteer suddenly let go of the strings that held him upright, Cabot slumped to the floor. "You look like an angel standing there," he said, his voice soft and raspy. Smiling a silly, pained grin, he held his hand out to her, and passed out.

ta

At first, everything was a fuzzy blur. *So. I've made it into heaven, after all,* he decided, grinning crookedly. *Why else would everything be white? And why else would there be an angel standing beside me?* He wondered if he'd see Maggie and Lindy soon. His mom and dad. They were all up here. It could be a regular family reunion.

He blinked, swallowed, tried to sit up and get a better look at heaven and at the angel. But the pain in his side stopped him.

"Now, you stop that," the angel ordered. "Lie still or you'll pop your stitches."

Stitches?

She'd placed both hands on his shoulders and held him down. He hadn't realized angels possessed such physical power. But then, he guessed, it took a lot of strength to fly from heaven to earth and back again, maybe dozens of times a day.

"You sure know how to scare a girl," she said. "You've been unconscious for hours."

He thought the angel sounded a lot like Elice.

She fluffed his pillow, then pulled the sheet higher on his chest, and the slight pressure made his side ache. He moaned softly.

"Oh, I'm so sorry. I'll get a nurse."

She turned to leave, but he grabbed her hand. "No. Don't leave me alone up here just yet." He closed his eyes and frowned, wondering why they'd need nurses in heaven. "Boy, am I thirsty," he said.

The angel held a blue plastic cup near his face, then guided a straw between his lips. Her hands were shaking. *Well, what d'ya make o' that?* he asked himself, taking a sip of the cool water. *Angels get nervous!* Grinning, he said, "I don't get it. My mama told me people don't want for anything up here."

He'd closed his eyes, then opened them at the sound of her laughter. *What was so funny?* he wondered. But even the angel's laughter, softly musical and sweet, reminded him of Elice. He'd been in heaven only a short time. Hours, the angel had said, yet he missed Elice desperately. The pain in his side didn't begin to compare to the ache in his heart for, if he really was in heaven, it meant she was down there, alone and unprotected.

"Cabot," she said, "drink some more water. You don't want to get a fever. If that happens, they won't let you go home."

Home? Cabot closed his eyes and tried to concentrate. He'd always assumed that once you got to heaven, you were there to stay. Confused by the possibility of a return trip, he opened his eyes and tried to focus. Was he in heaven or not? Nothing made sense. He felt like a man lost in a fog. And then a deep voice said, "Mr. Murray, I'd like to ask you a few questions, if you feel up to it."

St. Peter? he wondered.

"He's heavily medicated," the angel explained to St. Peter. "Don't pay any attention to that silly grin on his face." She stuffed another pillow under Cabot's head. "There. Is that a little better?"

Cabot nodded. He could see a door, and beyond it, a hallway. There had been a song in the seventies called "Stairway to Heaven." He wondered if he'd missed one called "Hallways in Heaven." The thought made him grin, and soon, the grin became a chuckle. But his merriment didn't last long, because laughing hurt.

The man with the deep voice came closer. He wasn't wearing white, Cabot noticed. He saw the badge first, reflecting the bright overhead lights. Then he recognized the navy blue uniform. This guy wasn't St. Peter. He was a policeman. *Cops in heaven?* Cabot thought. It seemed even funnier than nurses up there. He stifled the laughter that threatened his side.

"Did you recognize your attacker?" the policeman asked.

"I. . .tried," Cabot answered, "but. . .couldn't get the . . .mask off."

"He was wearing a mask?"

Cabot nodded. "Ski-type. . .black knit. . .red trim around the eye and. . .mouth holes."

The officer scribbled on the small tablet balanced on his palm. "Mrs. Glasser has filled me in on the events that transpired prior to this attack."

He didn't understand why this officer needed to be told what had happened; didn't heavenly beings just automatically know such things? But he started to talk, anyway, and the story tumbled out, from the moment he first heard the footsteps, until he watched the shadowy figure disappear on the other side of New Freedom Road. The officer appeared to have gotten every word down on his little pad, nodding and frowning as his pen scratched the white pages. He thanked Cabot for his help, and then he was gone.

"You look tired, Cabot. I think you should try and get some sleep."

"Don't need sleep in heaven. But then, you're not supposed to feel pain in heaven, either. And my side hurts a lot."

She giggled at that, and gently touched his shoulder. "You're not in heaven, you big nut. You're in the hospital."

Hospital? Cabot ran a hand through his hair and blinked with confusion.

"The doctor said you could go home tomorrow morning," she explained, holding his hand. "But you'll have to stay with us for a few days. We have to keep an eye on that wound so it won't get infected."

Haven't been in a hospital since. . . .

"But even after you're allowed to go back to Foggy Bottom," she continued, "you won't be able to do any heavy lifting. That means no farm work. Maybe we ought to call Walter. . . ."

. . .since the day Maggie and Lindy died. There had been no angel to greet him upon awakening that day. Suddenly, he was very sleepy. "I'm glad I'm not dead," he mumbled. "Even if it means I'm not in heaven."

He heard her giggle again, and kissed the hand that still rested on his shoulder. "I love you," he said, his voice raspy with exhaustion.

The last thing he saw before closing his eyes was her angelic smile, and Cabot took her wonderful words with him into his dream world: "I love you, too."

❧

He insisted that the couch would be a perfect bed. "Besides," he said, "I can watch the ball games from here."

"Don't be silly. Your feet will forever hang out of the covers."

"Cooler that way. I don't want to be stuck back there, all by myself."

She shot him a maternal, scolding look. "Well," Elice said, arms folded over her chest, "the doctor did say he wanted you up and about a couple of times a day. I guess you could sleep in there at night, and rest out here during the day."

"I won't take your bed from you—"

In the voice she reserved for the kids, Elice said, "Fine, then. We'll just haul you back to the hospital where they're accustomed to dealing with uncooperative patients."

She wasn't smiling. Without words, Cabot agreed to be agreeable.

Elice let Wally borrow her car twice a day so Cabot's animals would be fed and watered on schedule. The rest could wait until he was better again.

His stay at Glasser Memorial turned out to be rather pleasant, after all. Elice, his ever-attentive nurse, saw to it he had plenty to eat and drink and provided games and books to entertain him when the Orioles weren't playing baseball. And then there was the added bonus of three round-the-clock playmates. Within days, he took meals at the kitchen table with them. He found himself regretting the day when he'd have to return to Foggy Bottom.

On his last night at Twin Acres, Cabot sat in the old brown chair in the corner of her bedroom, watching as she flapped fresh, line-dried sheets onto the bed. "When are you going to marry me?" he asked.

She'd been stuffing a pillowcase, and her hands froze midair. Turning slowly, she met his eyes. "You're not kidding, are you? I half expected to see that teasing grin plastered all over your face."

He loved that wonderful smile of hers. "Stop stalling and answer the question, Elice." Cabot watched her cheeks redden, watched those brown eyes blink rapidly, and watched her swallow, hard, then resume her bed-making. She was smoothing the quilt when she said, "Okay. Time for you to—"

It startled her when he put his hands on her shoulders and turned her around. "You're not gonna get out of this one, pretty lady. I'm not letting you go until you answer my question. When are you going to marry me?"

When she looked at him like that, he wanted to stop time, because he'd never seen more love directed at him. He'd never loved anyone more; never would love anyone more. It hurt a little, admitting that, because he didn't think it possible to love a woman more than he'd loved Maggie. But the proof was right there in his arms.

He wanted to say it again, but he'd said it so many times that week, he was beginning to sound like a broken record. Instead, he settled for a long, sweet kiss.

"Yuck," Danny said, leaning on the door frame. "Mush. Right here in my own house."

Cabot half expected Elice to pull away, to flush with embarrassment, to try and explain the embrace—and the kiss—to her son.

"That's what you get when you don't knock," she said instead.

"Door wasn't closed," Danny said, his playful grin telling them both that he was pleased to see the warm exchange between his mother and his new buddy. Snickering, the boy repeated, "Yuck. You're never gonna get better if you keep that up."

Cabot laughed and said, "They don't make any better

medicine, Dan."

⁂

Wally had practically moved into Foggy Bottom. He'd mowed the lawn twice and trimmed the hedges in front of the farmhouse. And Cabot's animals seemed more contented than ever. Cabot decided that a cash payment couldn't repay the man for all the extra things Wally had done in his absence. That's when he got the idea. He left a message at the Olsons for Wally to stop by Foggy Bottom as soon as possible, then got busy preparing his surprise for the old soldier.

Wally showed up at suppertime, knocked on the back door, and waited on the porch, twisting his Orioles cap in his hands. "C'mon in!" Cabot said, waving him into the kitchen. "I'm just about to sit down to a plate of canned spaghetti. Care to join me?"

Grinning and nodding, Wally sat across from Cabot. As they ate, they discussed their plan to protect Elice.

"Guess whoever has been pickin' on Miz Glasser got bored and started botherin' somebody else," Wally said. "When's the last time anything strange happened?"

Cabot held his side. He didn't verbalize his thoughts, but Cabot believed it too much of a coincidence that everything eerie stopped that night. Either the madman in the ski mask had been frightened off by the violence of what he'd done, or he was planning something even more vicious. Much as he hated to admit it, the latter was more likely, considering all the trouble the maniac had gone to to terrify them up until that night.

He gave Wally a slice of the peach pie Elice had baked and frozen for him. When the big guy finished, Cabot led him to the garage. "You took such good care of things around here," he began, opening the huge double-wide doors, "that

I didn't think a couple of measly bucks was payment enough." Standing aside, Cabot pointed at a shiny red convertible. He took Wally's hand, turned it palm up, and dropped a keyring into it. "That key starts the motor," he explained, poking the square-headed key, "and this one," he added, pointing at the rounded one, "locks and unlocks the trunk and the doors."

Wally met his eyes, confusion furrowing his brow.

"It's yours, big guy," Cabot said, gesturing toward the car.

It only took a moment for the information to register. "Guess now I'll need insurance," was all he said before he slid behind the steering wheel. He sat there fiddling with the radio dials, turning the headlights on and off, testing the air conditioner and the heater. Then he climbed out of the car and shook Cabot's hand. "I'd give you a hug," Wally said, grinning, "but I'm so excited I'd probably pop your stitches."

When he drove off, his smile was so wide that Cabot could see it when he turned onto Oakland Road. His own satisfied smile was still in place when he answered the phone the next morning.

"It's all over town, Mr. Murray. You're a local legend."

"Why?"

"It's not every man who pays his farm hands in cars," Elice teased. She paused, then added, "Everyone knew what that car meant to you."

"It was in my way. Since the only woman I'd ever consider marrying won't set a date, it doesn't make sense to stockpile useless metal."

"I never said I wouldn't marry you."

"I'll be right over. I want to hear this in person."

It normally took fifteen minutes to drive from his side of

Freeland to hers, but Cabot managed it in seven this time. He felt great, healthy and fit, happier than he'd been in ages. The nut who'd been after them must have decided they were no longer worth his trouble. Life was grand.

But when Cabot pulled into her driveway and saw the squad car parked where he usually put his Jeep, his heart began to pound. He slammed on the brakes and threw the car into park, then leaped from the front seat so fast he didn't even bother to close the door. He heard a man's laughter as he stepped onto the porch, then Annie's sweet giggle. Elice was standing just inside the front door, waiting to escort the officer out. "Thanks for stopping by," she was saying. "It's good to know you haven't forgotten about us."

She noticed him then, and her whole face lit up. "How'd you get here so fast? Did you trade the Jeep for a jet?" Suddenly, her smile faded and Elice grabbed his hands. "Cabot, are you all right? You're as pale as a ghost."

"I'm fine. Saw the—"

The officer joined them on the porch. "She's a real cutie," he said, tousling Annie's hair. "Don't you worry. We'll keep a close eye on you guys." He chucked the child's chin. "Wouldn't want anything to happen to this precious angel here, would we?"

Long after the police car was out of sight, Cabot's heart continued to race. Elice took him inside and sat him in the recliner, then handed him a glass of cold water. Sitting on the arm of his chair, she stroked his blond waves.

"Sorry I scared you," he admitted. "It's just that when I saw that squad car, I thought something had happened to you or one of the kids." He sipped the water.

"Do you intend to have a stroke every time you see a patrolman or a police car?" she teased.

Cabot rubbed his side. He wasn't smiling. "I keep

remembering that night. It could have been you—"

"But it wasn't."

He squeezed her hand, then remembered why he'd come over here in the first place. "So, you'll marry me, eh?"

She nodded.

"When?"

She shrugged.

"Soon?"

"Maybe."

"How soon?"

Another shrug.

"Now?"

"No. Not now. I'm in the middle of a sign job. And besides, it's time for lunch."

Cabot laughed and pulled her onto his lap. "Tomorrow, then?"

"Not tomorrow or the next day. . .not until you're completely well."

"I'm fine."

"That's why you're as white as snow."

"I'm only human."

She kissed his chin. "That you are."

"Aw, no," Danny moaned. "Are you guys at it again?"

Cabot laughed. "Dan, I think we're going to have to put a bell around your neck."

&

Oh, but aren't they just adorable? he asked himself, sneering sarcastically. Cabot and Elice made him sick with all their hugging and kissing. They'd even gotten those kids to accept the whole ridiculous scene. He hoped they enjoyed their little game, because it wouldn't last much longer.

Games had rules, after all, and since he made this game up, he could change them any time he pleased. Like he'd done that night.

Elice had always been so prim and proper. Such a well-bred lady. He'd gone over there only to put a little scare into her, so from then on she'd react with respect to his warnings. Imagine his surprise when he discovered Cabot spending the night!

Well, the ex-cop paid for his sin. Paid with a nice deep cut in his side and a big old goose egg on his head. The town gossips said he'd been laid up for weeks. And wasn't Elice Glasser a sweet one to take him into her home and nurse him back to health, they'd said. He'd proposed marriage, they added, and Elice had accepted. He wondered if they'd set a date. Wondered if they'd have a big wedding or a small celebration. Wondered where they'd honeymoon, which house they'd live in, his or hers.

She was a sweet one, all right.

Those three nice kids deserved better than that. They'd started out with a bum for a dad. And if Elice married Cabot, he decided, they'd end up with a bum again.

It was pointless, really, to wonder about their plans. He smiled. There'd never be a honeymoon because there would never be a wedding. Not if he had anything to say about it.

৯

They didn't let the rainy weather predictions spoil their plans but went right ahead with the barbecue. God must have sent Cupid to intervene, because it didn't rain a drop until they'd cleared the table. It had been a long, tiring day of playing volleyball and badminton. Annie had been yawning for the past half-hour when Elice said, "I'd better get them home."

"How 'bout if I stop by in an hour or so?"

"Haven't you had enough of me yet?" she laughed.

He drew her into a protective hug. "That day will

never come."

Cabot didn't wait quite an hour before heading out for Twin Acres. The kids were asleep when he arrived, though, and, as usual, they sat on the back porch, talking quietly.

"We were meant to be together," he said.

"Is that right?" she asked, grinning.

"Sure." He took her hand and led her into the yard. "Just look at all the patterns we've developed. Like sitting and gabbing for hours."

"And drinking Kool-Aid."

He sat on the wide wooden seat of the tree swing and patted his thigh. She accepted his invitation, slinging one arm around his neck, and holding the thick hemp with her free hand. Raindrops from the rain that had fallen earlier drizzled down upon them from the leaves above, dampening their hair, but not their spirits.

Cabot's big foot, planted firmly in the gravel beneath the swing, stopped their swaying. "I've never wanted anything more in my life than I want you."

His lips were fractions of an inch from hers when she said, "It'll be wonderful, won't it? Being married, I mean."

He kissed her. "Better than wonderful. Spectacular."

It began to rain again, and she started to run for cover. But Cabot caught up with her, stood in her path, and wrapped her in a huge hug. It wasn't a very important gesture, really, yet it seemed to change things somehow. Her lips softened under his, and she returned his kiss—really returned it—for the first time.

Cabot wanted her on every human level. It didn't matter that she wasn't a young thing, or that she had three kids to raise, or that she was stubborn and opinionated. She loved him, warts and all, and that was enough.

Elice ended the kiss and gazed deep into his eyes. He

saw the naked vulnerability in the brown spheres. Rain rolled down her soft cheeks and sparkled on her long dark lashes. "You're even gorgeous when you're all wet," he said, tightening his hold on her.

As if on cue, God issued forth a loud crash of thunder and a bright bolt of lightning. Elice hugged him, laughing. "See? He's listening, always. I warned you—"

"Isn't that comforting to know?" Cabot said wryly.

❧

Every weekend, Cabot brought the kids to Foggy Bottom. He and Elice had decided to move into the farmhouse after the wedding, since it was larger and sunnier. The more time the children spent there before the big day, the more quickly they'd adjust afterward. Their delighted squeals changed the atmosphere of the house, reminding him of how it had sounded when he was a boy. His mother would have loved to hear the happy voices of children in her kitchen again. So would his dad, for that matter. He hoped they were enjoying the scene from their places in heaven.

"When do I get to ride a horse?" Danny wanted to know. He'd worn his cowboy hat and capguns, just in case.

"After lunch, we'll saddle 'em up and head for the horizon," Cabot drawled.

"I don't want to sit on any stinky old horse," Annie said. "I'd rather stay here and play with the kittens in the barn."

"You can play with the kittens when we get back from riding," Cabot said. "But right now, I'm gonna rustle us up some grub, pardners. Y'all mosey on outside an' play till it's ready. Stay close by now, y'hear?"

Danny enjoyed Cabot's cowpoke talk, but the girls rolled their eyes. "I'll keep these fillies in line, Cabot," the boy said, sashaying toward the door.

It was going to be some life, Cabot knew, when they

became a real family. And it couldn't happen soon enough for him.

It hardly seemed like two months had passed since her house had been ransacked. She'd been grocery shopping. As always, she'd taken the kids. Cabot thanked God that Elice paid attention to details. Small things, like open doors that ought to be closed.

She'd known better than to go inside, and drove straight to his place instead, telling the children to wait in the car while she told him what she'd found upon arriving at Twin Acres: The intruder had broken a window to get into the house this time. But only Elice's room had been disturbed. The contents of every drawer had been rumpled, every shelf on the wall emptied. The clothes in her closet had been pushed aside, and the bed stripped.

Blue paper rested on her pillow. "It's not over till the fat lady sings," the note said, "and she won't be singin' at your wedding."

As before, the police found no evidence. They'd spent countless hours in her house, scouring for clues. Their man was smart, all right. Maybe a little too smart, Cabot hoped; self-confidence had been responsible for snaring more than one bad guy in the past.

❧

Since meeting the Glassers, Cabot had been collecting a lot of memorable moments. Christmas morning, in his opinion, was way up there on top of the list. After church, they headed home, where Elice prepared a delicious country breakfast, complete with homemade currant jelly. Only then did they gather in a small circle around the tree.

When most of the hooting and hollering died down, he went out to the Jeep and brought in a gigantic box. "It says 'Mom' on the tag," Emily announced, shaking it gently. "It might be huge, but it's not very heavy."

He'd spent an entire afternoon wrapping it, first in its original box, then larger and larger ones, and finally, in the container his new washing machine had been delivered in. When she finally found the smallest box, wrapped in silver paper and tied up with a red satin bow, she lay on the floor and pretended to be too exhausted to open even one more thing.

The children's groans brought her back to a seated position, and coaxed her to unwrap the last package. "You're a terrible tease," she said, grinning at him as she tossed the ribbon aside. Her mouth dropped open when she lifted the lid.

Cabot didn't know which sparkled more—her eyes, or the diamond in the palm of her hand. She sat in silence for several moments, simply staring at it. Finally, she moved to his side and put it into his hand. He immediately knew what she wanted, and got onto one knee.

"Will you marry me?"

That mischievous glint he'd learned to love so much lit her eyes. Giggling, she held out her hand. And as he slipped it on her finger, she whispered over her shoulder to the kids, "I hope it doesn't turn my finger green."

&

Bob Glasser played with the tackle box, the gift Cabot had given him, for nearly an hour. He put it down only because his wife insisted he could not bring it to the dinner table. He never mentioned that Sue was just as fascinated by the leather-bound copy of Kidnapped that Cabot had given her at Elice's suggestion. And he'd never have admitted that he couldn't wait to get home and put their gift to him, a recording of his favorite opera, *Aida*, on the stereo.

Dinner was a festive occasion. Cabot ate ravenously, much

to his hostess' pleasure. He'd been nervous about this day, because it was important. . .no, vital, that the Glassers like and accept him. Cabot yearned to be a member of a big, happy family. Bobby's parents were as eager to be accepted as to accept. He couldn't remember a brighter Christmas.

Back at Twin Acres, the children asleep, Cabot and Elice settled in the living room. He loved to sit across the room and peek over the top of the newspaper at her. He watched her sturdy little hands control the knitting needles, and he listened to the quiet clicking as the sweater she was making took form. She'd made the sweater he wore now, a bulky fisherman's knit. He didn't know when she had found the time to make it; had never seen her working on it. But he was quick to point out that it was one of the nicest Christmas gifts he'd ever received.

"How do you feel about two weeks from now?"

His question had cracked the quiet of the night and made her jump. "You made me drop a stitch. Shame on you." Then, smiling, she said, "What's two weeks from now?"

"A week before Father's Night, that's what."

She frowned and put her knitting aside.

"If we get married before Father's Night at school, I'd be more than just a father figure."

Her smile widened, but didn't quite make it to her eyes. "I thought we decided to wait until spring."

Cabot crossed the room in three huge steps and sat beside her on the couch. "I'm not made of stone, Elice."

"Well," she teased, "you can be pretty hard-nosed at times."

He ignored her grin. "Don't make fun of me. I'm serious. You made me promise to keep my distance. Well, I've kept my distance, and my promise. But let me tell you. . .it hasn't been easy."

She stared at her sparkling new engagement ring, but said nothing.

He took her hands in his. "If you love me, marry me!"

Elice withdrew her hands. "It's not that simple."

"It's exactly that simple." He took her in his arms. "It's Christmas," he said. "Forget that stupid promise I made, just for tonight."

She melted against him. "It's only Christmas for ten more minutes. I can bend the rules for that long, I guess."

They sat quietly for a long time, and then she said, "I'm glad you kept your promise."

"Why?"

"Because we appreciate this so much more."

"I've never been the kind of man who takes the good things in life for granted, Elice—"

"Shut up and kiss me," she said. Then, smiling, she added, "And make it a good kiss. It's nearly midnight."

❧

"What do you think I ought to wear?" Cabot asked on the afternoon of Father's Night.

"Your navy blazer and gray slacks, with that wine-colored tie," Elice suggested. "You look very handsome and sophisticated in that outfit."

Half an hour later, he called back. "Maybe I ought to rent a car. The Jeep's pretty beat up."

"No one's going to see it; it'll be in the parking lot."

An hour passed before the phone rang again. "What if someone wants to know why I'm at Father's Night?"

"You'll tell them you're the soon-to-be father of the Glasser group."

He was due to arrive at six o'clock; the phone rang at five-thirty. "Are mothers allowed?" he asked.

six

"Look, Cabot!" Annie squealed, pointing to a twig. "That tree has a baby!"

Leaning over to inspect the new shoot, he said, "Well, so it does."

"Where do you spoze it got a baby?"

"Maybe God thought the big tree needed some company."

She nodded her agreement. "God is like that."

As they walked and talked, investigating nature, Cabot knew he learned far more from Annie than he could ever teach her. He recalled the first time she'd seen the pond. It had been a steamy August day. That morning, a thunderstorm had turned the water dark and cloudy. "Yuck," she'd said. "Looks like a giant mud puddle."

"It's murky, all right," Cabot had agreed.

"Murky?"

Chuckling, he explained, "It's another word for 'yucky.'"

"Rivers have names. Lakes and oceans have names. I think your pond ought to have a name, too. I'm going to call it Murk."

Now, as he watched her walk along the frozen bank, Cabot grinned when she said, "It sure would be neat to skate on Murk."

Gently, he squeezed her mittened hand. "No, darlin'. It wouldn't be neat. It looks safe, I know, but it isn't. If you go out there, you'll fall through the ice." The vision of her, struggling in the freezing water, sent chills up his spine. He squatted and met her eyes. "You can never go onto the ice.

110

Not for any reason. It's very deep and very dangerous. You understand what I'm saying?"

She stared into his worried eyes, nodding, one blond curl bobbing from beneath her red stocking cap. "Okay. I won't go out there. I promise."

Cabot stood and lifted her into the air. "That's my good girl. I don't know what I'd do if something happened to you."

While he couldn't say he loved Annie more than the other two, Cabot had to admit he loved her differently. It had been Annie, after all, who'd opened the door to his own personal heaven on earth—Twin Acres. He kissed her cheek.

And she kissed his. "I love you, Cabot."

"Time for me to fix lunch," he said, putting her gently onto the ground. "Stay close to the house, so you can call Emi and Dan for me when it's ready."

She looked up at him, blue eyes overflowing with love. "Okay. I'll play with Cuddles."

He watched her skip toward the barn, where Cuddles the kitten waited for her new, two-legged playmate. Later, after the wedding, the tabby would become a family pet. For now, though, it remained a barnyard cat. At first, it amazed him how quickly Annie bonded with the little thing. Then he remembered how fast he'd fallen in love with Elice and all three kids, and the instant closeness made perfect sense.

He could hear her sweet little voice, jabbering to the kitten about the snow and Danny's treehouse and that she'd save a piece of chicken from her lunch for it. "Don't hide from me, you silly thing," he heard her say, "I love you!"

❧

It had been a mistake, breaking into her house that way, because instead of running from Cabot, as he'd expected, she'd run straight into the big ape's arms.

He'd been on the other side of the road, crouching in the underbrush, when her battered yellow Vega rattled into the driveway. She must have seen it the same moment he had: The open front door. He should have gone out the same way he'd gone in. Why had he been so careless?

Elice was a smart one, all right. Rather than go inside and face possible danger, she calmly and carefully backed the little car out of the driveway and pointed it in the direction of Oakland Road. . .and Foggy Bottom. That had surprised him, because she'd always been so independent, so sure of herself, strong-minded, and opinionated. Those things had been only a few of the reasons he respected and admired her as he did. He didn't know another woman like her and honestly believed no other such woman existed.

He didn't like picking on her. It was the hardest part of his plan. But how else could he teach her, once and for all, that the ex-cop wasn't the man for her?

Apart, they'd been so easy to torment. He'd deliver a well-timed note or place a telephone call, then stand back and watch the excitement. Lights would go on, shadows would race back and forth in front of the windows, agitated voices would rise in pitch and volume. It was wonderful.

Together. . . . Well, those few times he'd tried scaring them when they were under the same roof didn't net the expected results. Quite the opposite. It seemed no matter how terrifying his trick, if he struck while they were together, whatever he did only brought them closer. The turmoil and mayhem, rather than blowing them apart like a mental grenade, bonded them. Like that super glue stuff, he thought, grimacing.

What galled him most, though, was the way her eyes glittered when she looked at the big ex-cop. She'd never looked at him that way. Not when he gave her flowers. Not when he invited her to parties. Not even when he brought trinkets for her kids. Sometimes he wondered what he saw in her at all. And then she'd smile that sweet smile, or say something kind, and he remembered.

Now, as he stood in the pines on the other side of the pond, he watched Cabot and Annie. You'd think they were a real family already, he glowered. It's enough to make a man gag.

It seemed to him that Cabot spent more time with Annie than with the other kids. He seemed to listen more closely to what she said and watch more carefully what she did. He'd heard in town that Cabot's little girl had died in the same car accident that killed his wife. Obviously, in Cabot's heart, Annie had become the daughter he'd lost.

His fingers and toes were growing numb from the near-freezing temperature. Moments ago, he'd considered heading home. But watching them gave him his best plan of attack yet. When he finally did leave, the weather and its accompanying temporary physical discomforts were the last things on his mind.

They would notice his absence if he didn't get back soon. And he couldn't have that. Alibis were all-important to him these days. As he drove the bright red vehicle toward his jobsite, he pictured her: Tiny, warm and kind, beautiful. He blinked away the pleasant image. Can't afford to go soft now, he chided himself. She'd knotted the rope the day she let the dumb cop put that engagement ring on her finger.

A small part of him understood what had motivated the commitment. She'd been scared, and being linked to Cabot by the promise of marriage made her feel safe. But it didn't make their closeness easier to bear.

Still, it had all worked out in his favor in the end. Their oneness had been directly responsible for the false sense of security that surrounded them. He remembered the night when, slinking around the shrubbery beside her dining room windows, he saw the cozy little setting—Cabot at the head of the table, Elice at the other end, passing out slices of cherry pie. When they'd finished eating, the kids happily followed suit as Elice led them in a harmonious rendition of "There'll Be Peace in the Valley." He'd made a decision, right then and there, and had been on a single-minded mission to make it real ever since.

If it were the last thing he ever did, he'd put an end to the peace in their valley. Maybe then he could learn to live without her.

જ

"I brought you these, Miz Glasser," said Wally.

"Where did you find such pretty flowers in the middle of winter?"

He blushed, scratched his curly gray head, and said, "I found a five-dollar bill in the parking lot over at Nardi's. I bought 'em at the store."

"You've brightened my day," she said, taking them from his extended hands.

He stood there, twisting his Orioles cap, and grinned. "The lady called them silk flowers."

"Very practical," Elice said, smiling. "They'll never die."

Wally beamed, then asked, "Have you seen Cabot yet today?"

She glanced at the wall clock. "He'll be here any minute."

"Good. He borrowed my typewriter a couple of weeks ago. I need to get it back. I got a card from a friend today. He's in the hospital. I wanna write to him. An' my handwriting is horrible." Wally laughed.

Elice swallowed. "I didn't know you could type, Walter."

He nodded. "Learned in the army. Before they sent me to Korea, I was a clerk for a whole year."

Her heartbeat had doubled, remembering Cabot's original suspicions about Wally. "Where'd you get a typewriter?"

"Found it in Mr. Olson's shed. He told me I could have it."

Elice dialed Cabot's number. Facing the wall allowed her to hide her doubt from Wally. "If he hasn't already left," she said, putting the receiver to her ear, "I'll ask him to bring it right over." *Walter has nothing to do with what's been happening to us,* she told herself as Cabot's phone rang. And by the time he answered, she'd more or less convinced herself she was right.

All the way over to Twin Acres, Cabot thought about her icy tone. He'd talked with her less than an hour earlier; she'd seemed fine then. Cabot supposed she'd connected the fact that he'd borrowed Wally's typewriter with the accusations he'd made that day in her kitchen. He'd never told her that he'd gone over to Wally's and "grilled" him, as she'd put it. And he hadn't mentioned what he'd discovered up there in the big guy's small apartment—that the crooked *e*'s in the notes and the *e* on Wally's typewriter matched, exactly. The moment Wally left with the typewriter, she lit into him.

"All right, Kojak," she said, tapping one foot. "Start explaining."

He didn't leave out one detail about that visit to Wally's. He watched her big eyes grow bigger with shock and disbelief. But before she could defend her friend, Cabot added, "For your information, I agree with you. The better I get to know him, the more I realize he couldn't be responsible for anything that's been going on."

Blinking nervously, she licked her lips. "But then

someone used his typewriter to write those notes. . . ."

Cabot hesitated. Elice considered Jack a friend, too. He didn't want to rile her tonight by spelling out what he thought of his old high school chum, because tonight, he intended to persuade her to set a wedding date.

"It must be someone he knows well," she continued, frowning as she paced the length of the kitchen, "because Walter doesn't have much to call his own. If he'd let someone have the typewriter. . . ."

Then she stopped dead in her tracks and stood up straight. Grinning, she said, "If someone had told me all this was happening to them, I'd think they were a little, you know . . . ." Her forefinger drew tiny circles beside her temple.

Chuckling, he agreed.

"I'm glad it's over. These past few weeks have been so wonderful, so calm." Her face brightened and she grabbed his hands. "See? I've been praying for a happy ending. And God answered!"

He held her close, partly because having her there was a comfort, and partly because he didn't want her to see his face. She was so intuitive and intelligent that she'd have known instantly that he didn't think it was over. Far from it. Cabot believed, without a doubt, that it had only just begun.

Gradually, the tranquility of the past few weeks had put the sparkle back into her eyes. She hadn't been this relaxed since. . .since they met.

"Isn't the Lord wonderful?" she said, hugging him tighter. "Look at all He's done for us! I don't think I've ever been happier."

Cabot kissed the top of her head and sighed sadly. At that moment, setting a wedding date was the farthest thing from his mind.

⤫

The next morning, stirring sugar and milk into his coffee, Wally smiled. "I like Miz Glasser," he told Cabot. " 'Specially lately."

"Why lately?"

" 'Cause she's always smilin' and laughin'. Just like in the old days. It's good to see her that way again."

"I know what you mean."

"Do you think we'll ever need to put our 'plan' into action?"

Cabot frowned. "I'm not sure. Doesn't seem that way right now, but that may be exactly what he's hoping we'll think, so we'll let our guard down."

Wally took a sip of his coffee and nodded. "Can't be too careful where Miz Glasser and those kids are concerned," he said somberly.

"Maybe we got lucky; maybe having you spend all that time at Twin Acres scared him off."

Wally put the mug onto the table, hard. "I wouldn't ever want to hurt anybody, Cabot. But if somebody tried to hurt her while I was around. . . ." The blue eyes narrowed dangerously. "Well, I don't know what I might do."

Cabot liked him. And he trusted him, too. Elice would always be safe in his presence, because Wally was the type of man who'd lay down his life for a friend. "She's lucky to have a friend like you."

He flushed. "I'm the one who's lucky. She's been good to me." Then, after a moment's hesitation, he dug in his pocket and pulled out a large pocket knife. "I found this while I was weeding under her bedroom window yesterday," he said, placing it on the table. "Is that the knife you got stabbed with?"

Cabot pulled out the blade. "Did you wipe it clean?"

Wally shook his head. "Never even opened it."

"Well, there's not a trace of blood. And from what I remember, that knife wasn't the retractable kind." He turned it over and over in his hands. "Maybe this one is Dan's."

Wally shook his head again, harder this time. "No way. Miz Glasser would never let him play with anything sharp. She's a good mother."

Cabot nodded in agreement, then closed the knife and placed it on the table. The men sat there, staring silently at the thing for a long time. Then Cabot thumped it, sending it spinning in a dizzying circle on the table top. He thought Wally seemed agitated. He'd never seen him looking so distraught. "Did you stop by this morning to show me this, or was there another reason?"

Wally leaned back in the chair. "It gave me the creeps. I wanted to see what you thought."

"Gives me the creeps, too."

"What will you do with it?" Wally asked, watching Cabot open and close the blade again.

He'd clamped his jaws together so tightly they'd begun to ache. Then Cabot relaxed and tried to smile. "I'm not sure. But let's keep this between us, okay? This could be nothing. I wouldn't want to scare Elice for no reason."

Wally stood and headed for the back door. "No, sir. Don't want to see that look on her face again. Not ever."

Cabot watched Wally drive off in the shiny red car. The big guy had changed, somehow, in the months Cabot had known him. He seemed keener, smarter, a little more sophisticated. Chuckling as he climbed into his Jeep, Cabot remembered feeling the same way when he drove the convertible.

❧

Cabot heard Elice's laughter first, then his. And when he

walked into the room that evening, his heart nearly stopped at the sight of them, sitting across from each other at her kitchen table, mugs of coffee and a plate of cookies on the table between them.

"Howdy, Cabot," Jack said, tipping an imaginary hat. "How's tricks?"

"Fine," he said, warily. He didn't smile. "You?"

"Same."

She greeted Cabot with a peck on the cheek. "Jack brought us a surprise," she said. "Pie filling."

"I'll admit I had an ulterior motive," Jack said. "Figured if I brought her the fixings, she'd be obliged to whip me up a pie." He winked at her. "She hasn't baked for me in quite a while."

Cabot's left brow rose high on his forehead. "Is that so?" He helped himself to a cup of coffee and sat between them at the table.

Jack leaned back, prepared, it seemed, to stay forever. "Leecie here invited me to supper." He winked at her again. "And this old bachelor has been craving some of her home cookin', let me tell you."

Cabot didn't like the possessive way Jack looked at Elice. The man didn't belong in this house. Something ominous shrouded him. Something that tainted everything around him. He'd liked Jack once upon a time, but right now, Cabot felt anything but friendly toward his former schoolmate, who sat there smugly sipping coffee and making small talk as if he were a frequent and welcomed visitor.

What Cabot had intended as a short visit turned into a long, dreary evening. First supper then dessert then conversation afterward. He'd left a lot of chores undone. But he wasn't about to leave Jack alone with her. He'd stay until next New Year's if that's what it took.

"You were very rude," Elice scolded when Jack finally left.

He didn't respond. It was true—he had been rude.

"He's been bringing us dented cans from the factory since Bobby died," she said, putting the last clean dish into the cabinet. "He's just trying to be helpful, Cabot. He knew it was hard for me at first."

Cabot pocketed his hands and stared at the toes of his boots.

"And Jack knows that you and I are engaged now."

The muscles of his jaw flexed in anger.

She frowned. "He says he's happy for us—"

"I'll just bet he is." The bitter edge to his voice hung heavy in the air.

Elice sighed. "He's a friend, Cabot. That's all he's ever been, and he knows it."

Cabot felt foolish, making such a big deal out of it. But a nagging sense that something horrible was about to happen struck when he saw Jack in her house, and it didn't leave, even after Jack was long gone.

She smiled sweetly. "You have no reason to be jealous. Jack's not my type."

Forcing Jack from his mind, he returned the smile. "Oh, yeah? What's your 'type?' "

Elice pretended to be deep in thought for a moment, then said, "Tall. Strong." She stood beside him. "Handsome," she added, "with curly blond hair and almost-brown eyes. Someone who does a horrible Kojak imitation. That's my type."

He forced a brave, friendly smile, but nothing she said made him feel any better. The little kiss that had punctuated her statement and the tender hug that followed it didn't improve his mood, either. Not even her admission of

undying love erased the sense of doom that Jack Wilson
had delivered to Twin Acres, disguised as pie filling.

≈

Cabot didn't know how many times the phone had rung
before he had heard it. He'd been up half the night, replay-
ing every smart-alecky word Jack had said earlier at Elice's
house. When he had finally dozed off, Cabot had slept
deeply and soundly.

"Cabot Murray?" asked a gruff voice.

"Yeah."

"Detective Sergeant Murray, of the Chicago Police
Department's Homicide Division?"

He read three-fifteen on the alarm clock's dial. "Do you
have any idea what time it is!" Cabot growled, propping
himself up on one elbow.

"You mean you don't recognize my voice? I'm crushed."

The voice was familiar, but Cabot couldn't put a name or
face with it just yet. "Whaddaya want?" he demanded
angrily, sitting on the edge of the bed now.

"Just passing through," the familiar voice said, "and since
your home town is just a hop, skip, and a jump from Baltimore, I thought it'd be rude not to pay my respects."

The voice was strangely familiar, but Cabot couldn't put
a name or face to it, so he decided to try out an old trick:
"You're not welcome here, Deitrich."

A pause. Then a brittle snicker filtered through the phone
and into Cabot's ear. "So you do remember me. I'm
touched."

Cabot wanted to hang up, but didn't dare. A few more
minutes of scrutiny, and he'd be able to identify that voice.

"I'm headin' south at first light. I only came east to settle
up with a fella who owed me."

Cabot ignored the implied threat. "That was pretty

stupid, Deitrich, breaking out of prison with only two years left to go."

The crazy snicker again. Then, "Two years is a long time in a place like that."

The guy was crazy, all right, but he wasn't Hawk Deitrich. Deitrich hadn't escaped. He'd been legally released from prison months ago.

"Why not call Judge Bollinger back in Chicago," Cabot said, still testing. "Let him know you're not interested in carrying out those death threats. You never know when you might need a couple of character witnesses."

"Who says I'm not interested?" he said. And without so much as a by-your-leave, he hung up.

Cabot stared at the receiver for a long time before replacing it in its cradle. He went into the dark kitchen and stood at the sink, staring into the yard as he sipped cold milk from the carton.

An hour later, still unable to put a name or face with the voice on the phone, Cabot got dressed and headed for the barn. It was nearly daylight, anyway; an extra hour or so would almost make up for the time he'd lost last evening at Elice's, babysitting Jack Wilson.

The phone call haunted him as he went about his work. He realized that anyone who'd ever watched television cop shows were convinced that cops, responsible for the imprisonment of criminals, received occasional death threats. The caller had been banking on that, hoping to throw Cabot off the trail.

He could have been one of those ex-cons who'd threatened Cabot. Slim possibility, but a possibility nonetheless. But it was definitely not Hawk Deitrich. Because a convict who forgets the name of his sentencing judge was a changed man, indeed.

Besides, Judge Bollinger didn't even exist.

⋙

Northern Maryland's heaviest snows accumulate in mid-February. That winter, Mother Nature took her work especially seriously, six times causing traffic jams and school closings in a two-week period. Like every kid in Freeland, Elice's children took full advantage of the extra play time, molding the fluffy white stuff into snowmen and snowballs and snow forts. When they ran out of building space at Twin Acres, they decided to move the freezing construction activities to Foggy Bottom.

On the first Saturday of the month, Elice got an order to create several signs for a local insurance company. She stayed home to catch up on her work while Cabot and the children headed for the farm.

Too impatient to wait for the others, Annie headed straight for the barn, calling Cuddles' name. Danny shouted that he planned to climb the big forked tree near the pond, where he'd built a treehouse last summer. And Emily announced that she'd rather stay inside and read beside the woodstove.

Cabot looked out the windows occasionally, checking on Annie and Danny. As he watched them scamper through the snow, giggling and squealing with delight, he smiled, pleased to know they enjoyed his place so much. It wouldn't take them any time at all to adjust to living here once he and Elice were married.

He watched Danny inch his way higher into the big tree, then settle himself inside the plywood cube he'd designed and constructed from scraps he'd found in Cabot's shed. Below him, Annie headed for the barn. Satisfied the two were safe and happy, Cabot settled into his easy chair, waiting for the chicken noodle soup Elice had sent over with the kids to heat up. He'd barely cracked the sports page when he heard the terrified screams.

"Cabot!" the voice shrieked. "Hurry! Get out here!"

Not taking time to step into boots or slip into a jacket, Cabot reacted to the panic-stricken cries and bolted outside without even closing the door behind him.

"What's going on?" Emily wanted to know as she ran behind him.

"It's Annie," Danny shouted. "She went toward the man. He had Cuddles. . . ."

Looking in the direction Danny pointed, Cabot saw a gaping hole in the ice, just a few feet from shore. Emily saw it at the same time, and immediately began to sob. He headed for the barn, and both children ran alongside him.

"I was up in the tree," the boy explained, crying harder than ever. "I told her to stop. I told her to stay off the ice. But she wouldn't listen. She was too busy listening to the man."

Cabot grabbed a rope from the peg beside the barn door, then headed for the pond. Despite Emily's and Danny's pitiful wails, he'd never heard a more deadly silence. Cabot couldn't take his eyes from the jagged hole in the pond, where a soggy red mitten clung to the ice.

He tied one end of the rope around a tree trunk. "Call 911!" he hollered as he tied the other end around his waist. "Tell them there's been a drowning. That'll get them here fast." Then, with no regard for his own safety, Cabot crashed through the ice.

Fortunately, Annie had fallen into the only shallow spot the pond had to offer. As he splashed around in the frigid water, he prayed with all his might: "Please, Lord, let me find her. Guide my hand to her." When Cabot's nearly frozen fingers felt a solid object, he formed a numb fist, held tightly, and pulled hard. Soon he could see the wet pink material of Annie's parka. He sloshed out of the water, holding her close, trying to warm her with his own body heat.

His heart pounding with fear, he stumbled toward the house, clutching her limp body against him. He hoped he'd reached her in time. It seemed like she'd been under the dark, cold water for hours instead of minutes; seemed like miles from the pond to the house instead of yards. He had to get her inside, where it was warm. His breaths were ragged and his mind confused when finally he reached the back porch.

Tears oozed from the corners of his eyes as he gently lay Annie on the floor near the woodstove. He pinched her tiny nose and began breathing into her mouth. Listening for the sound of his breath to exit her lungs, he prayed harder: "Not Annie, too, Lord," he said. "Not Annie."

He heard the sirens, but continued to force breath into her until the paramedics arrived. Then he and Emily and Danny huddled in the middle of the room.

"Is she going to die?" Danny sobbed.

Cabot hugged them tighter and whispered, "She can't."

❧

The paramedics hadn't wanted the extra passenger, but they wanted a wrestling match with Cabot even less. He sat on the floor between the two narrow cots, holding her tiny hand, his cold, wet clothes clinging like a second skin. One of the paramedics draped a blanket around his shoulders. Cabot didn't seem to notice.

At the hospital, when he insisted on remaining at Annie's bedside in the emergency room, an orderly threatened to strap him into a chair. "Stand back and let the doctors and nurses do their jobs," he said, then disappeared around the corner. Someone handed Cabot a large styrofoam cup of hot, black coffee. Another kind soul guided him to a hard, white chair. "Put these on," the orderly said, handing him a set of dull green surgical scrubs, "before we have to sign you in as a pneumonia patient."

Mechanically, Cabot obeyed, and changed in the tiny bathroom just outside the E.R. He wondered how Elice would react to the news of the accident, wondered how long it would be before she'd arrive, hoped Annie could hold on until then, and prayed Elice wouldn't hate him.

Seated in the stiff-backed chair once more, he waited and listened and watched as the white-garbed professionals efficiently tended to Annie. An hour slipped by as he sipped the coffee, Danny's words echoing in his head: "She went to the man. She went to the man. She went to the man." What man! Cabot demanded of no one.

"Mr. Murray," said a soft voice. "You can see her now."

He jumped up so fast, the coffee splashed on the doctor's garb he'd borrowed. "Is she all right?"

"Still unconscious, I'm afraid," the nurse said, pointing at the second pastel-curtained cubicle in the E.R.

He'd expected it to be bad, but Cabot hadn't been prepared for this. Annie looked like a little robot with all those tubes and needles and hoses connecting her to the beeping, humming monitors. Standing at her bedside, he held her tiny hand and brushed a strand of flaxen hair from her forehead. "Look at you," he said, stifling a sob. "The nurses have put a nightie on you. It's got blue flowers all over it. Blue, Annie. . .your favorite."

No response.

"Your mom's on the way," he added, sniffing. "Wake up, now, so you can show her your pretty pajamas."

She didn't open her eyes or smile or giggle. Not one precocious remark came from the blue-gray lips.

"Hey, darling," he said, hot tears burning his eyes, "sing 'Rock-a-Bye' with me." Cabot swiped at a tear that rolled down his cheek. "C'mon. . .wake up and sing for me."

"She's in a coma, Mr. Murray."

Cabot faced a pair of bespectacled, somber, brown eyes. "I'm Dr. Cummings," he said, extending his hand.

Cabot ignored it, trying to make sense of the doctor's words.

Dr. Cummings put his hand back into his large white pocket. "It might be brief, or we could be in for the long haul. We have no way of predicting, since we don't know for certain exactly how long she was deprived of oxygen."

Cabot swallowed, then glanced at Annie, pale and lifeless. "But she'll be okay, right? She won't die?"

"I wish I could tell you what you want to hear, Mr. Murray," the doctor said quietly. "But at the moment, I honestly don't know. I'm sorry."

Cabot squared his shoulders. "She's going to be fine," he said. "She's going to wake up and be her old self any minute now."

The doctor sighed. "Well, we can hope."

Cabot felt weak, lightheaded. He slumped into the chair beside the bed. His broad shoulders lurched with each sob, and the dry, racking sounds of his misery echoed throughout the small cubicle.

"I'll be on this floor for another half-hour or so," the doctor said, backing out of the room. "If she moves, even the slightest, have me paged."

Cabot scooted the chair closer to the bed and sandwiched her tiny hand between his big ones, then began singing Annie's favorite song: "Hush little baby, don't you cry . . . ." His voice trembled, but he forged on. "Daddy's gonna sing you a lullabye. . . ."

He noticed warmth, a slight pressure on his shoulder, and turned to look into Elice's eyes.

"I'm so glad you're with her," she whispered through her tears. "I'm so glad you're here for me." Elice slipped her arms around him and leaned her head atop his. She held him that way for a long time.

≈

They'd been at her bedside more than twenty-four hours, Cabot pacing, Elice praying. But Annie hadn't come to yet. Obviously, it wasn't a day for miracles.

Dr. Cummings made several visits during the night, studying Annie's chart, shining his little light into her eyes, taking her pulse, and reading the printouts from the monitors that clicked and beeped and hummed relentlessly. He spoke no words of hope, showed no sign of encouragement. His manner, while kind and professional, indicated certain doom. "You need to get out of here for a while," he suggested to them. "It's important to keep up your own strength; you'll need it if there's a change."

Cabot looked at Elice closely. She hadn't cried, not since those first harrowing moments after she'd joined him at the hospital. "The doctor is right," he said. Taking her hand, he led her to the cafeteria, where he purchased two sodas and two bologna and cheese sandwiches.

"She's in God's hands now," Elice said when he slid the tray onto their table. "There's nothing we can do but wait and pray."

Her voice had lost its vitality, yet she sat there, composed and calm, fully expecting God to intervene on Annie's behalf. It was a dangerous game she played, Cabot thought. A game he'd played himself years ago. . .and lost. Elice had always been a strong woman, but Cabot knew that the death of a child required much more than emotional strength.

He didn't know what, exactly. He only knew he didn't possess that magical, secret character trait, because losing Maggie and Lindy had nearly killed him.

He'd tried hard to fight his disbelief. Everything he'd learned his whole life told him that his doubts were wrong . . .sinful. But in the end, after he'd gone through the motions of pretending to be brave, honesty won out.

Everyone experiences grief differently, his pastor had told him. For some, he'd said, memories of the deceased became a lifeline. Cabot had been a father, a husband. Then suddenly, with no warning, he was a man alone. For him, memories were not helpful, and grief was a bitter heart that blamed the Creator for his solitary lifestyle.

"It'll pass," the pastor had said. "You're angry now, and that's normal. But the Lord will forgive your anger, because He understands. He lost a son, don't forget."

The pastor had been right. Time dulled the raw edge of Cabot's pain. But doubt is a strange, reverberating, haunting thing, for though he knew he'd been forgiven, Cabot couldn't make himself believe again in a Being that allowed such agony to touch the innocent. First He had allowed Maggie and Lindy to suffer a painful death. And now Annie, pure as a newborn, lay just out of reach of Death's cold hand. Cabot wanted to know where God had been when she walked onto the ice. Where He was now that she teetered between life and. . . .

"Danny asked about you when I called home," Elice said.

Her words startled him back to the present. Cabot remembered how upset Danny and Emily had been earlier. "How's he doing?"

"He blames himself."

Cabot met her eyes. "What?"

"He said if he'd been faster. . . ." She stopped talking and swallowed the tears that threatened to choke off her words. Elice sipped her coffee, then continued. "I told him if he hadn't been in that tree, Annie wouldn't be alive at all. But he wasn't having any of it."

Her smile, feeble though it was, warmed his heart. "He's a lot like you that way," she said.

Cabot nodded. "I'll talk to him. Set him straight."

She touched his hand. "What would I do without you?"

Cabot grimaced and pulled his hand from beneath hers. *You'd do a lot better,* he thought. *You'd be safe and calm and happy, like you were before I came into your life.*

"I know what you're thinking," she said, waiting for him to meet her eyes before she continued. "You're blaming yourself, just as you've been doing over every little thing that's happened." She took a deep, shaky breath, and squeezed his hands between her own. "It's not your fault. None of it. Especially not this."

He couldn't meet her eyes.

Elice touched his cheek. "You saved her life," she said. Then, the awe she obviously felt echoed in her voice: "You saved her life!"

He stared past the cash register, over the heads of other hospital visitors, beyond the staff members who filled empty food bins and restocked shelves. If Annie didn't make it, what difference did it make that he'd saved her? Unless she woke up, able to enjoy life as she had before, what had he accomplished, really?

Besides, the awful truth gonged too loudly to be denied: The man in the pines, the writer of the notes, the destroyer of their peace was one and the same person, acting out some dark, demented need to avenge something he believed Cabot had done to him. He could handle that, alone, but watching them suffer. . . .

"I love you," he heard her say.

Cabot felt the sting of tears behind his eyelids again. He'd turned her tranquil life into one of torture and torment, and now, on top of it all, he'd become a full-time sniveling weakling. How could she love a man like him?

"Drink your coffee, Cabot. It's getting cold."

He nodded and took a sip. *Get a grip,* he told himself. *She needs your strength right now. She deserves a man she can lean on.* So he blotted his traitorous eyes and blew his nose on a paper napkin and sat up straight. He'd be brave and strong. . .for Elice.

Whatever he did from here on out would be for her.

Because he honestly didn't care what happened to himself any more.

☙

Cabot worked on his bravado all the way over to Twin Acres. If he didn't put on a good show, Danny would continue feeling responsible for Annie's accident. He couldn't have that, since every horrible thing that had happened to the Glasser family since he'd returned to Freeland had been his fault.

When the boy greeted him, Cabot noticed his tentative smile and red-rimmed eyes. Hugging him, he said, "How's my boy?"

"Fine." The boy's shoulders slumped from the burden of his grief and guilt, and he refused to meet Cabot's eyes.

Cabot looked across the room at the picture of Annie on the mantle. Her smile, sincere and sweet, beamed out at him, and his heart throbbed. He cleared his throat. "So, what's all this nonsense about you feeling like it's your fault that—"

Danny broke away and flopped onto the couch. "It *is* my fault."

Cabot sat beside him. "You're a hero, Dan. Why, if you hadn't been up in that tree, Annie would be dead right now."

Dead. Annie would be dead. The words chilled him.

"If anyone is to blame," Cabot continued, "it's me. I should have been out there with you guys. I never should have allowed her to play—"

"You're the hero, Cabot. You're the one who jumped into the pond and saved her."

Cabot forced a grin. "So it's a tie, then. It's not your fault, and it's not my fault," he lied, "and we're both heroes." He hated lies and fibs and half-truths but, at times, he believed, they were necessary. This was one of those times. At least now, the blame had shifted from Danny's little-boy shoulders to some unknown place. In Cabot's mind, though, the lie had been exactly that: He'd carry the guilt and blame for the rest of his life.

❧

There were plenty of things he'd done in his past to be sorry for, but this topped them all. He'd sunk mighty low to have used a little girl that way.

He didn't have anything against her. She was a pretty little thing. Every time he'd seen her, she'd reminded him of a storybook princess. Too bad she, like her mother, had swallowed Cabot Murray's lines. So it was more the cop's fault than his. Murray had pushed him into doing it.

The newspapers were having a field day at his expense, calling him a maniac, a madman, a lunatic. If they knew the whole story, the true story, they'd realize he wasn't any of those things. Angry, maybe, but then he had a right to be. Cabot Murray had cost him plenty.

Perhaps he'd send a bouquet of flowers to the hospital. That would show them he wasn't heartless. Maybe he'd buy Annie one of those great big teddy bears he'd seen at the York Mall. Or maybe he'd get both. That would prove he wasn't such a bad guy after all.

He'd show them.

He had feelings, too.

seven

"Look what I brought for you today," Cabot said quietly. The candy bar slid easily from his shirt pocket. "Remember the first time I brought you one of these? It was the day after we met." He sat on the chair beside her hospital bed. "You got chocolate all over your mom's skirt." Chuckling softly, seeing it in his mind, he put the candy into the nightstand drawer with the rest of the gifts he'd been bringing Annie since she fell into the pond.

"How 'bout if I read you a story?"

When he picked up the book of fairy tales, the teddy bear caught his attention. "Where'd this come from?" he asked the silent sleeping child. Cabot lifted the envelope that lay beneath the huge brown bear and opened it. As he scanned the message, his hands shook violently and his heart began to beat hard. Cabot ran into the hall and headed straight for the nurse's station.

"Who delivered this to Annie Glasser's room?" he demanded, holding the stuffed bear in midair.

"A man delivered it first thing this morning," said the nurse.

"He put it into her room himself?"

She nodded. "Said he was an old family friend."

"Did you get a name?"

She shook her head. "I was on the phone when he came in. Sorry."

Cabot's fear turned to fury. "What did he look like?"

She winked. "Not bad. Not bad at all."

133

"Describe him," Cabot snapped.

The nurse stood taller, and frowned with annoyance at his tone. "He was tall. Very tan. With one of those Marlboro Man mustaches."

"Dark hair? Light hair? What!" Cabot demanded.

"Lots of hair. Curly, and dark brown." Her voice was cold and unemotional now.

He'd made her angry with his ceaseless questions and aggravated tone. Cabot tried to sound a little gentler. "Have you ever seen him before?"

She smiled at that, and winked again. "I'd remember if I had. He was quite a handsome fellow."

Cabot lifted the receiver of her telephone and put it into her hand. "Call the cops. Tell them to get down here right away. Tell them they're going to need to post a guard outside Annie's door, because that 'handsome fellow' is the guy who tried to kill her."

Back in Annie's room, waiting for the police to arrive, Cabot read and reread the note, typed on that same blue paper, complete with the tilted *e*'s. "Get well fast," it said, "so you can give your new friend a nice name."

His eyes moved to the bed and settled on Annie's pale face. That guy had been here. Right here in this room, looking at her, possibly touching her. What psychotic message is he sending now? Cabot wondered.

He believed Annie could hear him. Believed that comatose patients were aware of everything around them. "Annie, darlin'," he said, "you're gonna get better. I'll see to it if I have to spend every minute right here at your side."

Cabot insisted on a police guard. He'd marched straight into the office of the chief of police and demanded that Annie be protected. In the end, once he learned Cabot had been a cop in Chicago, the chief agreed. Satisfied once the uniformed officer was in place outside her door, Cabot rode the elevator to the hospital's first floor. It took a moment to find the door he'd been searching for. Inside the quiet room, he sensed peace.

Kneeling at the rail, Cabot folded his hands and bowed his head, hoping God wasn't too angry at him to hear his plea. "I know it's been a long time since I've admitted it," he began, "but somewhere deep inside, I still believe You can do anything.

"Maggie and Lindy. . . . That was an accident. It took a while, but I accepted that. What happened to Annie. . . . That was deliberate, and we both know it. I can't accept that."

Cabot hid his face in his hands, then focused on the crude wooden cross that hung on the wall above the altar. "Help me find the guy," he whispered to the Man hanging there. "We can't let him get away with this. We can't let him hurt anybody else."

❧

For two days and two nights, Cabot stayed at Annie's side, leaving her only long enough to spend a few moments in the chapel. He had no proof that his time there did any of them any good. He only knew that being there gave him hope, and he hadn't had hope in a long time.

He'd seen the guitar at the nurses' station on his way to the first floor earlier. Cabot had read to Annie until he was hoarse. Surely she was as tired of hearing the same old stories as he was of reading them. "Mind if I borrow that for a few minutes?"

The nurse handed him the instrument. "No rock and roll, now," she warned, grinning. "We've got sleeping people up and down these halls, don't forget."

His melody wafted gently around Annie's room, changing

the stark, sterile atmosphere into homelike warmth. "Hush little baby, don't you cry," he sang. It was her favorite song, and she'd made him sing it every time he tucked her into bed. "Daddy's gonna sing you a lullaby." After hearing it several times, she'd learned the words, and had begun to accompany him. She loved to sing. Once she'd figured out how good she was at it, she sang things that ordinarily would be spoken: "Danny's got his shoes on the co-ouch," she'd tattle. Or "Mommy's got paint on her fin-gers."

". . .If that diamond ring don't shine," he continued, "Daddy's gonna buy you a silver mine."

"Where's Cuddles?"

His hands froze and the singing stopped. Cabot thought he must be losing his mind, for he could have sworn he heard her speak.

"Did she get lost in Murk?"

Cabot looked at her. At the sleepy, but open, clear blue eyes.

"I don't know how that man got her," Annie said, her voice hoarse from days of silence.

"Don't look so sad," she told him. "It's not your fault Cuddles got dead."

The hazel eyes glistened with tears. "Darlin'," he said, "I'm not sad. I'm the happiest man on earth to see you awake. That was some nap you took!"

Her smile, weak though it was, brightened the entire room. "I'll be right as rain in no time," she said. "You'll see."

He'd taught her that one-liner. It made him grin.

"What's in your pocket today?"

He leaned the guitar against the nightstand and pulled a box of crayons from his shirt pocket. "I know how much you like to color."

A grin curved her pale lips. "I'm going to color you a

beautiful guitar."

Hugging her tenderly, Cabot chuckled.

"Know what I wish?"

"What do you wish, darlin'?"

"That I could climb into your pocket."

He laughed and sat back, and looked into her sweet face. "Now, why would you want to do that?"

"Because. . .it's always so full of love."

&

Annie spent another week in the hospital. Keeping her in bed those first few days at home had been hard work for Elice, Emily, and Danny, for she wanted to run and play as if nothing had happened.

Cabot watched her closely, looking for signs that the underwater experience had permanently damaged her. Gratefully, he acknowledged that she'd been spared even the slightest scar.

It was Elice who worried him most. She'd never been a heavyweight but, since the pond incident, she'd lost a good ten pounds. She blamed her dark circles on Annie's recuperation, saying she'd been sleeping with one eye opened, listening all night in case the child might need her.

But Cabot knew better.

While they were doing the dishes together one evening after supper, he asked Emily, "How's your mom these days?"

She shrugged. "She's okay, I guess."

"She looks tired," he said.

Emily sighed. "She cries a lot in the night. But I know she sleeps some, because she has bad dreams."

Cabot took her hand and led her to the table. Seating her on his lap, he tucked a lock of hair behind her ear. "Tell me about them."

"Well, I think she dreams about the man who had Cuddles

that day. She hollers at him. And she hollers at Cuddles. She won't let any of us out of her sight for a minute. She must think he'll come back. That he'll try to hurt one of us." She paused. "Do you think so, Cabot? Do you think he'll come back and hurt one of us?"

Cabot closed his eyes, unable to face Emily's scrutiny. "Of course not," he said. If they gave an award for telling convincing lies, he was sure to win it. But he summoned even more conviction into his voice, just in case. "Definitely not."

Emily got up from his lap and headed for the door. "Maybe you ought to tell Mom that."

He didn't know where the thought came from, but St. John the Baptist, the church where he'd worshipped as a child, came to mind. The place was miles away, but when he left Elice's that evening, he headed for the quaint little chapel.

Seated in the last pew, his eyes fixed on the large, stained-glass window behind the altar. In colorful gleaming shapes, Jesus stood in the Garden of Gethsemane, arms and eyes raised to heaven, beseeching the Father to hear His last prayer. Cabot got up, walked slowly to the front of the church, and fell to his knees.

He had a lot to be thankful for. Annie hadn't merely survived. . .she was her old self again. Danny and Emily had accepted him as a permanent part of their lives. And Elice loved him, still, despite the pain his past had brought her.

Yet he felt lost, alone.

Worse, he felt guilty.

The Sacred Heart beamed down from another stained glass window, a symbol of suffering and love. Mary smiled gently upon him. Joseph's understanding eyes met his. The crucifix edified Christianity.

And he thought of Elice, who hadn't been sleeping.

Of Emily, who worried about her mother.

About Danny, who tried so hard to be a man, long before his time.

And Annie, who'd nearly died because of him.

He stood there in the church of his youth, knowing full well what he must do.

"When the police catch the guy who's been terrorizing them," he said to his found-again Friend, "I'll pack up and move on. I'll get out of this place before anyone else is hurt."

Cabot waited and listened for a silent blessing. A sign from God that he'd made the right decision. Getting no visible or audible clue from the Creator, Cabot stood. He left the church, convinced that his decision had been blessed by the Almighty.

He wasn't the first human to make the mistake of second-guessing God.

&

Every day Wally spent hours at Twin Acres, weeding, mowing grass, running errands. At the end of a long, spring afternoon, he stopped at Foggy Bottom on his way home. "Miz Glasser isn't happy any more," he confided to Cabot. "I think she misses you."

Cabot had been avoiding her since making his decision. "You're good to go over there and help her out," he said.

"Jack's been helping, too," Wally said. "If he's not on the phone, he's stopping by."

The news made every muscle in his body tense, though Cabot couldn't explain the reaction. It was no secret that Jack liked her. Everyone in town knew he'd set his cap for her long before Cabot returned to Freeland. But Jack had more or less kept his distance since that night at the carnival—until now.

"What do they talk about?" Cabot asked.

Wally snickered. "You oughta visit more, Cabot. Then you'd hear for yourself." Twisting his baseball cap, he added, "Mostly, she talks about you."

"Me? She talks to Jack. . .about me?"

Wally nodded. "She tells him she can't understand why you stopped coming around. Yesterday Miz Glasser told him she never loved anyone more. Said she didn't know what she'd done to offend you."

He hadn't meant to cause her pain. In fact, Cabot had given it a lot of thought. Short and sweet and to the point, he'd decided, would be the least painful way to end it. "Next time my name comes up, just tell her I'm busy."

"Tell her yourself," Wally said, grinning as he imitated Cabot's straightforward mannerisms and voice.

Cabot couldn't help smiling. "Maybe I'll just do that," he said.

❧

It was like the proverbial snake! Cabot felt lucky not to have two fang prints as a result of overlooking the obvious. If only he had some proof.

"Hey, old buddy," he said into the phone, "how's life?"

Jack didn't speak for a long time. When he did, he said, "What do you want?"

"Well, it's like this, Jack. . . . I got a letter from my insurance company today. Seems they want to raise my rates. And I'm going to dash off a hot letter, and let them know I won't stand for it. But I want it to look professional, so they'll know I mean business. Trouble is, I don't have a typewriter. Maybe I could borrow yours?"

"I don't have a typewriter."

"Strange. I could have sworn I heard Wally say you'd mailed a typed letter to *the Baltimore Sun*. A letter to the editor, I think she said it was."

"Oh, that." Jack remained silent for a moment, then added, "I borrow Wally's machine when I want to type something. It's not much, but it's better than nothing."

Cabot felt the heat of adrenaline race through his heart the moment Jack stopped talking. "Well, thanks for the tip, pal. You take care, now, y'hear?"

He sat there, rubbing his chin for a minute or two, wondering if his call had elicited the expected reaction. Right this minute, he hoped, Jack was planning retaliation. He'd have to be an idiot not to know that Cabot suspected him.

When three uneventful days passed, Cabot began to think maybe he'd given Jack too much credit. Maybe he'd been such a good actor that Jack hadn't seen through his ruse. He remembered the day he paid Wally a visit.

"I need to have a look at your typewriter," he said the moment Wally opened his apartment door.

"Sorry. Jack stopped by this morning and took it home."

Cabot's fists clenched and his jaw tensed.

"What's wrong? You look strange."

He looked at Wally. "Can I trust you with some very important information?"

"Sure!" Wally closed the door and pulled out a chair for Cabot. "I'm good at keeping secrets. You know that."

Cabot took a seat at the kitchen table. "I know who tried to kill Annie."

The blue eyes widened. "Who?"

"You can't tell a soul. If any of this got back to the wrong person, it would be very dangerous for Elice and the kids."

Wally made the Boy Scout salute. "I swear. It'll be our secret."

Cabot took a deep breath. He was taking a big chance, telling Wally everything, but he had no choice. If he hoped to prove his suspicions, he couldn't do it alone. With Wally's help, Cabot could get the information—and the evidence—that would ensure a long prison term for Jack Wilson.

"Ever notice that your typewriter has a crooked *e*?"

Wally shook his head.

"Well, the *e*'s on notes Elice and I received are exactly like the ones on your machine."

"I didn't do it!" Wally sounded as wounded as he looked.

"I know that. Someone who borrowed your typewriter did."

His brow furrowed. "Mr. Olson," he said, holding up one finger. "You," he added as another finger popped up. "And. . . ."

The blue eyes brightened and he inhaled deeply.

"And Jack," Cabot finished.

Wally's frown deepened. "But why would he want to hurt Annie? Jack told me once he loved Miz Glasser. That he'd marry her if only she'd let him. Why would he do something like that to her if he loves her?"

Cabot sighed, shrugged. "I haven't a clue, Wally, but we have to stop him before he does any more damage. We might not be so lucky next time."

The blue eyes darted to the place where the typewriter usually sat. "He even borrowed my paper." He looked angry now. "Do you think he wanted her to blame me?"

Cabot followed Wally's gaze to the stack of blue paper on the tiny table beneath the window. He nodded. "And we're going to let him go right on thinking you're responsible. That'll keep him off guard. His next mistake will cost him his freedom."

❧

Wally came running into the barn at Foggy Bottom. "He was over at the Glassers'," he said, trying to catch his breath.

"I saw him. I saw what he did."

"Calm down, Wally." Cabot draped an arm around his shoulders. "Let's go inside. You can tell me all about it."

"It was a long time ago," Wally began as they walked toward the house. "It was in the summer. I was having supper with the Glassers. I didn't want to go home, so I sat under the kitchen window afterwards. I went around to the living room then, and sat in the bushes over there."

Cabot only nodded.

"I fell asleep, and a noise woke me up. I saw somebody running away from the house. Running across her back yard. The next day, she found that note."

Inside the house, Cabot poured Wally a tall glass of cold water and gestured toward a chair. As the big guy gulped the water, Cabot thought of the calculations he'd made before Wally showed up.

"I could see something shiny in the dark," Wally began. "I saw him running, then he stopped and stood beside the shed for a long time. He had on a cowboy hat, so I couldn't see his face. But there was enough moonlight that I could see his belt buckle. It was silver. And big. And it had a red stone in the middle of it."

Cabot sat across from him, leaning forward, testing his patience so Wally could tell his story without interruption.

Wally ran his hands through his hair and moaned. "I wish I wasn't so dumb. If I had remembered this before, maybe Annie wouldn't have been hurt. Maybe none of that stuff would have happened."

"Remembered what, Wally?"

He looked deep into Cabot's eyes. "I see that belt buckle all the time. Nearly every day, lately. I didn't realize it until he brought back the typewriter. It was Jack's belt buckle."

It wasn't much. But it was all they had.

❧

It was sketchy at best, the D.A. told Cabot. And with Wally's mental condition and reputation in town, it wasn't likely his testimony would be weighed with much seriousness. Cabot had never been more frustrated. He knew that no matter how long the arm of the law grew, it couldn't reach all the dark and ugly corners of a mind like Jack Wilson's.

Well, he would come up with more proof. He'd find another piece of evidence that would prove, without a doubt, that Jack was not only unstable and dangerous, but capable of committing every act of aggression that had tormented the Glasser family.

Wally kept his word and didn't tell a soul that Jack was Cabot's prime suspect. He made one mistake, though, perhaps a fatal one.

Elice had sent him to Nardi's for milk and eggs. While he stood at the cashier's counter, Marge asked how Annie was these days.

"She's fine," he said. "And I know who hurt her. I can't tell you his name, but I know who he is."

"You do?" Marge gasped. "How would you know a thing like that!"

"Me and Cabot figured it out. And we're gonna fix him good, too. When we catch him, I'll go to court and tell the judge what I saw that night." He stuck the baseball cap back on his head. "He's gonna spend a long time in jail for what he did, that's for sure."

Marge shook her head and handed Wally the bag of groceries. "Be careful with that," she said, grinning. "Elice doesn't want scrambled eggs this late in the day."

Wally laughed. "I'll be careful."

His confidence had grown considerably since he'd been

helping Cabot. He took greater pains with his appearance and paid more attention to his grammar, too. Everyone had begun to notice the new Wally—including the shadowy figure that came out from the bread aisle after the big guy drove away.

"Will that be all today?" Marge asked.

"Yup. Just the bread."

"Haven't seen much of you these days, Jack. You find yourself a pretty lady to chase?"

He made himself return her smile. "I've been busy," he said, handing her a five-dollar bill, "that's all."

"Well, don't be such a stranger," she said. "I miss seeing that handsome face of yours."

He grinned crookedly, picked up his bag, and pocketed the change. As he headed out the door, he sent her a flirty wink over his shoulder. And, as he revved up the motor of his shiny red truck and shifted into reverse, he decided the simple-minded fool would never testify against him. Because he wouldn't live long enough to take the stand.

ہ

It had been difficult to dial her number. Difficult to make small talk with Danny before the boy ran off to find his mom. She'd behaved as though they'd talked an hour ago, rather than nearly a month ago. Cabot knew her well enough to understand why: She'd done some heavy-duty praying, and God had no doubt informed her that because of all he'd gone through with Maggie and Lindy, he needed some time to put his life in order. And because she loved him, Elice was giving him that time.

"Maybe you and the kids can come for dinner after church on Sunday," he said, trying to sound jovial.

She'd responded immediately with a friendly, "We'd love to." Then, after a moment, she added, "We've missed you, Cabot."

He'd missed them, too. But that wouldn't change what he had to do. "Stop by at about two o'clock," he told her. "I'll whip up one of my specialties."

"Can I bring dessert?"

"Sure." He heard the pain and uncertainty in her voice. It broke his heart. "I'll see you Sunday, then," he said, and hung up.

He hated the awkwardness that existed between them now. Knowing that he'd single-handedly caused it didn't help matters. What they had would soon be a thing of the past, so he wanted this meal to be special. Something they could all remember with fondness. They deserved one pleasant memory of their time with him, he decided.

He planned the menu carefully, shopped thoughtfully. Once he'd put the groceries away, he started cleaning. He wanted the meal and the house to be perfect. That's what Elice was, after all.

She deserved perfection on their last day together.

&

He was pleased, when she arrived, to see that she'd lost that tired, withered look. Silently, Cabot thanked God. He knew he'd never be able to carry out his plan if she had continued to go downhill physically.

Elice wore a sweater, exactly like the fisherman's knit she'd crocheted him for Christmas, with crisply pressed jeans. Her chestnut curls framed her face like a halo. She was the best thing that had happened to him since he'd lost Maggie and Lindy. Cabot prayed he'd have the courage to carry out his plan.

All through dinner, she looked at him with that giving, loving expression. Years from now, he knew, when he closed his eyes, it would be that look he'd see.

How he managed to keep the conversation going as they ate was a mystery to him. Mostly, he admitted, he had the children to thank for that, with their nonstop chatter and never-ending questions. He was glad he'd invited Wally, too. The big guy loved family gatherings. Elice had been right, after Annie came home from the hospital, when she'd said that Wally was blossoming in their family atmosphere.

"I'm going out to pet the horses," Wally announced after dinner. The children grabbed their jackets and followed him into the crisp, spring sunshine.

For a moment, he lost himself in the past, thinking of the meals and laughter and happiness they'd shared in months past. Then he remembered the reason he'd arranged this meal, and the memory destroyed his blissful daydream.

She seemed to sense that something bad was about to happen, and jumped up to start collecting the dirty dishes. "Why don't you put your feet up and read the Sunday paper," she suggested, "while I wash up these dishes."

He stood beside her and took her wrists. "We need to talk," he said gently.

Her eyes, wide and frightened, reminded him of the terrified little fawn he'd caught in his headlights several nights ago. Cabot coaxed her back into the chair, then refilled her coffee cup.

"Things have been pretty peaceful lately, haven't they?"

Elice nodded.

"Do you know why?"

She shook her head.

"Because I haven't been around, that's why. I've been very selfish," he said, his voice softer now, "exposing you to all that misery, simply because I couldn't stand to live a day without you."

Her mouth formed a thin, angry line. "Are we back to

this again?" She took a deep breath, then let it out slowly. "You scared me for a minute there. I thought it was something serious."

He thought she was beautiful when she smiled like that. But Cabot wouldn't—couldn't—be dissuaded. "You're right. . .we've had this conversation before. But this time will be the last time. I've made up my mind."

She rolled her eyes and clucked her tongue. "Honestly, Cabot, I don't know what I'm going to do with you."

Cabot decided not to respond to her teasing. Rather, he stuck to his carefully rehearsed speech: "You're going to say goodbye. And then you're going to load the kids into the car, and go home, where it's safe and peaceful."

Elice's smile vanished like smoke, and the frightened doe-eyed expression returned. "What about you? What will you do?"

"Wally will run the farm for me. I'm heading for the mountains."

She began stacking plates again. "I realize that everything that's been going on. . .it's been hardest on you, Cabot. I think you deserve a vacation. How long will you be gone?"

He'd practiced this speech over and over. So why couldn't he just say it? "I won't be back," he said quietly, staring at the floor.

Elice didn't say a word. She seemed to be waiting for him to take back what he'd said. When he didn't speak, she slumped into a dining room chair and said, "I never blamed you for anything that happened."

She sat there, hands folded primly in her lap, her jaw set, her shoulders back. It was her "hold the tears back" stance, he knew, and he felt even worse knowing he'd pushed her this far. He held his head in his hands and prayed for the strength to do what must be done.

"I love you," she said softly. "You can't hide from that. No matter how far away you go."

Cabot sprung to his feet and stomped around the dining room. "I'm not hiding, Elice. I'm. . .I'm trying to guarantee your safety."

She stood, too, and carried a pile of dirty dishes to the kitchen sink. "By leaving me? You're ridiculous." Elice put the stack of plates onto the kitchen counter with a clatter.

"Maybe so," he admitted, "but I'm also dangerous."

Elice followed him, then stood in front of him and faced him head-on, hands on her hips, eyes blazing. "I never met anyone so full of himself in all my life! You're just a man, Cabot, with flaws and limitations, just like the rest of us. And here's a news flash for you—you're pretty easy to love, in spite of them!"

He tucked in one corner of his mouth. This wasn't going according to plan at all.

"You know that I love you, don't you?" she asked.

He nodded. He knew it like he knew his name. Like he knew the sun would rise in the morning and set at night, though he didn't deserve an ounce of it.

"Do you still love me?" she asked.

The question shocked him so badly that he answered without thinking. "Of course I do."

"Then I don't understand why you're running away."

"I told you; I'm not running away, I'm—"

". . .leaving because you're 'dangerous,'" she paraphrased, her voice thick with sarcasm. And then she laughed. "The man who sings children to sleep, and comforts them during thunderstorms, and cries at Disney movies. Dangerous, indeed."

Cabot frowned. "I'm leaving tomorrow. I've already

packed. My mind's made up."

"Well, I'm glad to see you're sure about something."

He couldn't talk to her when she was like this. She looked exactly as she had on the day he'd met her—self-confident and secure. She'd be fine. In a few weeks, she'd be back on track, getting on with her life. He didn't have to worry about her. Elice was the strongest woman he'd ever met.

"What will you tell the kids?" he asked.

"You needn't worry about them. They'll be just fine."

She'd implied, with her words and her tone, that the four of them were accustomed to being loved and left. He'd never live this mistake down. Not if he lived to be a thousand.

"But—"

"But nothing," she snapped. "If you really feel this strongly, well, then go already. I hope you find what you're looking for."

Suddenly, his decision no longer made quite so much sense. He knew he was the biggest fool on earth to even be considering walking away from a woman like this. "I'm not looking for anything—"

Elice moved closer to him and said, "Promise me something."

He couldn't have denied her anything, especially now.

"Write me from time to time, so I'll know you're all right."

Several moments passed before he could answer her. He'd have given anything to put his arms around her, hold her close, and whisper into her thick, soft hair that he'd never leave her. But he remembered that day at St. John's, when he'd presumed the Lord's silence was a blessing upon his decision to leave.

"I'll keep in touch."

"One more thing," she said, wiggling her forefinger.

Puzzled, he leaned closer.

She wrapped her arms around his neck and held him tight, then kissed him long and hard. "You'll get another just like it when you come home," she said, and shoved him onto the porch. "Enjoy your fresh air!" she said, and slammed the door.

Cabot stood there for a long moment, shocked silent by her outburst, amazed by her strength and determination. He couldn't help but grin—a woman as tiny as Elice had put him out of his own kitchen. Before his feet even hit the lawn, he knew he wasn't going anywhere, except maybe to buy a marriage license.

❧

The long walk around the pond cleared his head. He'd go inside and apologize, and promise never to be so stupid again. He'd make her set a wedding date, and they'd put this whole sorry business behind them. And if anything more happened, at least he'd be there to protect her. The decision felt good, felt right. Much righter than the one he'd made in the chapel. So much better, in fact, that he realized he'd misread God's signals.

Heading back to the house, Cabot heard a ruckus in the barn. Wally's voice, undoubtedly in pain, cried out above the sounds of frightened farm animals. "You can't get away with this," he shouted. "Cabot knows about you and—"

Wally's words ended so abruptly that Cabot's blood ran cold. He sneaked up to the window and looked inside. What he saw took his breath away. Jack had pinned Wally to the floor and was rubbing his face into the straw. "You're not going to tell anybody anything," he said through clenched teeth.

Cabot walked quietly around to the back of the barn where double, smaller doors overlooked the fields. Slowly, he lifted the wooden slat that held them closed. Silently, he opened one slightly and slipped through the small opening. Luckily, the stalls blocked him from Jack's view.

The metallic sound of a releasing pistol hammer echoed in the huge space. He'd been wearing the .32 ever since Annie got out of the hospital. Jack was a severely disturbed man, and Cabot felt he needed to be prepared for anything. He was glad now that he'd broken the promise he'd made to himself upon returning to Freeland. It had been silly, anyway, to vow that he'd never touch a firearm again. Guns and violence had been a part of his life for so long that Cabot should have realized he couldn't hide from it.

Cabot felt dampness between his palm and the pistol grip. He was ready for whatever lay ahead.

Jack's constant mumbling drowned out the sound of Cabot's cautious footsteps as he crossed the barn's floorboards. With only a wall of plywood between him and them, Cabot couldn't afford even one misstep. One mistake could cost Wally his life.

Easing nearer the edge of the wall, Cabot stood behind the big black mare. Jack's back was to him, his right arm arched high above Wally's head, a crowbar in his hand.

"Get into that stall," Jack hissed. "Hurry up! Before I use this on you!"

Wally's eyes seemed fixed on the weapon. He sat up and crab-walked away from Jack. It was as he stood that Wally noticed Cabot, standing beside the mare in the stall behind Jack.

Cabot pressed a forefinger over his lips and prayed the big guy would have the good sense to look away, before Jack could follow his gaze. Otherwise, he wouldn't be able to get around the horse and over the stall quickly enough to prevent Jack from hurting Wally further, and he'd be forced to use the .32.

His prayer was answered. Wally walked backwards, inching away from the stall. There was a vicious cut above his right eyebrow, and another on his lower lip. A huge bruise glowed on his left cheekbone, and both blue eyes were nearly swollen shut.

"I said get in there!" Jack demanded. He laughed then, and added, "It'll look like you scared the horse, and she stomped you. Let's see you sit in a witness box after she gets through with you."

Wally moved slowly, very slowly. "Why did you do it, Jack? Why did you try to hurt them? I thought you loved them."

The questions stopped him. Jack lowered the crowbar slightly. "He's taken things from me for as long as I can remember. My dad used to say 'Why can't you be more like Cabot Murray? Why did George get a son like that . . .and I got you?' "

Jack nearly let the iron slip from his hand. His massive shoulders slumped forward. "Job. Cars. Girls. Everything I ever wanted, he took from me. Even Elice."

Cabot used the moment well, and leaped over the gate. "Put down the crowbar, Jack," he said in low, even tones.

Jack spun around, but didn't seem at all surprised to see Cabot standing there, gun in hand, facing him. "Well, hello there, old buddy. When did you get here?"

"Put down the crowbar," Cabot repeated. "You don't need it any more."

In an instant, Jack whirled around and grabbed Wally, throwing the big man off balance. Jack got him in a headlock, and held the crowbar's angry teeth inches from his temple. "I don't think I want to put it down, Cabot. But you might want to put the gun down."

Cabot felt a bead of sweat slide down his spine. "You're already in enough trouble, Jack. Don't make things any worse for yourself."

The crowbar pressed into the soft skin beside Wally's eyebrow. "I'm not one of your Chicago crooks," Jack spat. "Show a little respect when you talk to me."

Cabot knew it wouldn't take much pressure to drive the crowbar into Wally's temple. He could squeeze off a shot, no doubt, and take Jack down. But Jack's reflex could kill Wally.

"You're caught and you know it," Cabot said. "Put down the crowbar."

Jack's dark eyes blazed with fury. "Not this time. This time, I win." With that, he began listing his grievances: "You and me were up for halfback in high school, remember? And the same job down at the quarry. We both wanted that convertible."

Cabot stood, quietly waiting for him to make a wrong move.

"Because of you, I didn't make the football team. Because of you, I didn't get the job at the quarry. You bought the car with money you earned on that job."

Jack tightened his grip on Wally's throat.

"But then you took Maggie, Cabot. She was my girl. But you came back in that pretty blue uniform and swept her off her feet. You killed her, you know. If she'd stayed here, with me, she'd still be alive."

The words, though Jack had whispered them through gritted teeth, plowed into Cabot's brain like a locomotive.

"But that wasn't enough, was it, Cabot?" In his anger, he'd increased the pressure of the crowbar, and didn't seem to notice the trickle of blood on Wally's temple. "It wasn't enough to have everything else I ever wanted. You had to come back to Freeland and take Elice, too."

Cabot had heard enough. "Put the crowbar down. You nearly killed Annie. You going for broke this time?"

Jack looked at Wally. The sight of the big man's blood seemed to frighten him for a moment, but his expression soon returned to a mask of dark vengeance.

Cabot watched the muscles in Jack's forearm tense. Cabot didn't have time to dwell on possibilities. He only knew that he had to save his friend. He took aim at Jack's right shoulder. The harsh crack of the gunshot reverberated in the barn, and the scent of gunpowder momentarily overpowered the sweet smell of hay.

Jack blinked, and the crowbar hit the hay-strewn floor with a thud. "You shot me. I can't believe you shot me." He slumped to the floor, moaning in pain.

Cabot didn't move, didn't breathe. He stood there, gun arm hanging limp at his side, the pistol dangling from his fingertips. "Are you all right, Wally?"

"Yeah. I'm fine." Wally wiped his temple. "It's not too deep."

Only then did Cabot notice her in the doorway. How long had she been there? How much had she seen?

The moment he met her eyes he knew: She'd seen it all.

He'd stared revenge in the eye more times than he cared to remember. The hateful glare haunted his dreams. But the fear and disappointment on her face was far more difficult to look at. He ached inside, knowing she wasn't afraid because of what she'd seen. Elice was afraid of him.

Maybe it was best that she'd seen him in action; seen the real Cabot Murray. Now she'd agree it was for all their good that he leave Freeland. She was on her knees, tending to Jack's shoulder wound when he realized it wouldn't be difficult now to convince her he didn't belong in her world.

eight

Elice had been kneeling beside Jack, dabbing his shoulder with the kitchen towel she'd carried into the barn. "He needs medical attention," she said, "and he needs it now. You must have hit an artery; he's bleeding like crazy."

It was her subtle yet polite way of telling him to leave. It wouldn't have surprised him if she'd spoken only after asking the Lord exactly how she ought to dismiss him. . .in the kindest, most Christian way possible, of course. Telling him to go inside and get help, he decided, had been God's answer.

But he refused to leave her alone out there. Even with a .32 caliber bullet in his shoulder, Cabot didn't trust Jack Wilson. "You call the ambulance," he told her. He hadn't budged since he'd fired the shot. "And call the police while you're at it."

She looked at her blood-soaked hands, then met his eyes. "You could have killed him." Her voice trembled, and her eyes, wide and bright with tears, blinked nervously. "Where did you get that gun?" she wanted to know.

Jack took her hand, nudged the diamond engagement ring on her finger. "He's evil, Elice. Evil and violent. He's not good enough for you."

"Nobody's good enough for her," Cabot snapped. "Not me, and certainly not the likes of you."

Jack closed his eyes. "Maybe you're right for once," he rasped.

Elice stood, held her bloody hands in front of her, then at

her sides, in front of her again, as though the vital fluid that had flowed from Jack onto them was a deadly concoction of some kind. She looked at Jack's shoulder, at the gun in Cabot's hand, at Wally's battered face, at her bloodstained hands again. Taking a deep breath, she closed her hands into tight fists, as if the action might hide the awful, sticky mess. When she saw that it didn't, she met Cabot's eyes. "You have to keep pressure on that wound," she said, "or he's going to bleed to death." Then, without another word, Elice fled from the barn.

She hadn't closed the door behind her, and Cabot stared at the huge, empty opening. Sighing heavily, he shook his head. It was over now, once and for all. He could, with a clear conscience, leave Freeland. That day in the cemetery, standing between the twin headstones that marked the graves of his wife and daughter, he thought he'd never live a harder day. He'd been wrong. Leaving Elice would be just as hard—harder, maybe.

"I'm going inside and see if Miz Glasser needs any help," Wally said.

The big man's voice reminded him where he was. . .and why. "Good idea," Cabot said. "Make sure the kids don't come out here. They don't need to see this." Using the gun as a pointer, he indicated Jack.

Once Wally was gone, Cabot looked at the gun. Clicking the safety into place, he tossed it aside. It landed with a quiet thump in the hay.

"What do you think will happen to me?" Jack asked.

Cabot walked over and crouched beside him, found the last clean spot on the towel, and pressed it against the bullet hole. "I don't know," he said truthfully.

Pale now from loss of blood, Jack winced in pain. "How many years do you think I'll get?"

Cabot shook his head. As always, Jack was concerned only with himself. That he'd caused Elice and her kids many months of terror never occurred to him. That he'd nearly caused Annie's death never crossed his mind. Certainly that he'd taken Cabot's last chance for happiness didn't enter his head. "Shut up," Cabot said, disgust ringing in his voice.

"I'll never make it if they put me in jail," Jack said, opening his eyes. He was having trouble focusing, and squinted hard, trying to look Cabot in the eye. "Don't do this to me, Cabot." He leaned forward, bent one knee, and planted a booted foot on the floor, seeking the leverage to stand. "I'll be okay. It's just a flesh wound; you've seen injuries like this before. . .this one's no big deal, right? I can leave. I'll go to Mexico. To Alaska, maybe. Don't turn me over to the cops. Don't let them put me away."

Cabot grimaced. "I put a .32 slug into you, Jack, and it blew your shoulder apart. You're bleeding like a stuck pig. You wouldn't make it to the Pennsylvania border."

Jack grinned a little. "But. . .Pennsylvania is only three houses up the road."

"Exactly. You'd be dead before you left Maryland."

He thought about that for a moment before asking, "Think she called the cops yet?"

Nodding, he said, "Elice is your friend, you fool. In spite of everything, she wouldn't want you to suffer."

Jack relaxed again and closed his eyes. "You're not a bad shot, considering you're a little out of practice."

That made Cabot grin a little. "Coming from you, I guess that's pretty high praise."

The men's eyes locked in silent battle for several moments. "I don't suppose I'll be welcome at the wedding. . . ."

Being reminded that it was over between him and Elice wiped the grin from his face. "There isn't going to be any wedding."

Jack inhaled. "I guess it's true what they say, then."

Confused, Cabot's brows furrowed. "What do you mean?"

"Every cloud has a silver lining," he said, and passed out.

❧

The cops took Cabot's gun and the one spent shell they'd found on the barn floor, and the paramedics took an unconscious Jack. Cabot carefully inspected Wally's injuries and, satisfied he'd suffered no permanent damage, advised the big guy to go home and get some rest. Once Wally was gone, he climbed into his Jeep.

"Wait, Cabot!" Elice yelled.

If he didn't waste time, he could start the motor and be gone before she reached the vehicle. Cabot didn't know what he'd say to her; he surely didn't want to hear anything she had to tell him right now. "You could have killed him," she'd said in the barn. He believed he'd see that horrified look on her face for a long, long time.

"Where do you think you're going?" she asked, her hands resting on the track of the open window.

Cabot stared at the steering wheel. "To hitch up the trailer, and head on out," he said quietly.

She was silent for a long time, and then she said, "I distinctly heard that policeman say you should make yourself available." Though he wasn't looking at her, Cabot knew her well enough to hear the smile in her voice when she added, "He sounded like a sheriff in an old western, telling the bad guy, 'Don't leave town.'"

So, she'd finally accepted the facts, he thought. She'd opened her eyes and looked long and hard, and seen him for what he really was—the bad guy.

"They know where to find me if they need me."

"But. . .what if I need you?"

He looked at her then. Standing there beside the Jeep, she seemed smaller and more fragile than ever. "Jack was right," he said. "I'm not good enough for you."

She looked off in the distance, up into the sky towards her house. It startled him when she grabbed his collar, and Cabot jerked back slightly. "If you say so. But remember this: I've always thrived on a good challenge." She pulled him close and kissed him, long and hard, before releasing his shirt and taking a step back.

Cabot sat there, stunned, blinking in confusion.

"Well, what are you waiting for?" she asked, hands on her hips. The inner turmoil made him dizzy: Half of him was relieved that she'd finally seen the wisdom of his decision to leave. The other half grieved that she'd stopped trying to talk him out of it.

"Go on," she said, waving him away.

Couldn't she see his heart was breaking?

"Because the sooner you leave," she added, "the sooner you'll be back."

☙

The place looked horrible, and putting it into some semblance of order filled the lonely hours of that first empty day. He wondered how long it had been since he'd been up there. Ten years? Fifteen?

Cabot poked the logs in the tiny woodstove, the cabin's only source of heat, and squinted at the hot, glowing coals. The radio's morning weather report predicted warm, sunny weather for Baltimore and vicinity, but up here in the mountains, they'd be lucky to see sixty-five degrees. And that early in the day, temperatures rarely climbed past forty-five.

Standing in front of the wide picture window, Cabot surveyed the grassy knoll below him. He and his father had built this dwelling, board by board. They'd started construction just before Cabot's tenth birthday and drove the last nail shortly after he turned thirteen. The place had seen plenty of good times, having been the gathering place for several generations of Murrays. Until yesterday, the only tears shed inside the little building had been cried by small cousins and nieces and nephews, inspired by bee stings and snake sightings and fish that got away.

On the other side of the window, Ragged Mountain soared heavenward, the cloudless blue sky surrounding it like mother love. His dad had often said he didn't understand how anyone could say they didn't believe in God, especially after they'd witnessed the awesome beauty of the vast mountain landscape.

Cabot turned from the view. It wasn't that he didn't believe; his deep, abiding faith had been the root of all his doubts. He'd been raised to believe that no matter what stumblingblock life put in his path, the Lord would show him a way around, over, or through it. He'd never questioned that. He had accepted life's disappointments as easily as its rewards, because he understood that God knew what was best for him.

But when Maggie and Lindy had died, Cabot had felt as though his whole world had stopped spinning. He had held onto police work like a drowning man clings to a life preserver. The constant, daily reminders that the earth was overpopulated by willful, evil beings had only underscored the doubts that had begun chipping away at his faith on the day he had lost them.

With his "Nothing ventured, nothing lost" motto set firmly in his mind, he had left Chicago, determined to live out his life alone. It had been a difficult decision, and it had been a big heartache that caused him to make it. After nearly five years as a solitary man, all it had taken to make him see how wrong the decision had been was a five-foot, hundred-pound bundle of energy called Elice.

The Lord knew what He was doing, all right. It seemed no matter what Cabot did, or where he was when doing it, he thought of Elice. Only one activity could blot her from his mind—prayer. Cabot had been praying a lot since arriving at the cabin. He had his solitary life back, and he had his God. What more did he need?

Coffee mug in hand, he stepped onto the narrow porch. A gentle rain had begun to fall, pattering on the leaves above and splashing quietly into the little stream that ran alongside the cabin. He took a deep, cleansing breath, then sipped the strong, hot brew. Smiling sadly, he remembered their parting scene. By now, surely she'd accepted how wrong he was for her. One painful fact echoed in his heart and mind: As wrong as he was for her, she was exactly right for him.

Cabot sighed and put his mug on the flat, wooden railing, and stared across the expanse of mossy grass at the wild rosebushes that grew on the hillside beyond the cabin. Elice would love them, he thought, picturing her flower-studded yard. She'd love the huge, majestic trees and the sparkling stream and the narrow, winding path that led deep into the thick forest. She'd love the deer that feasted on wild berry bushes, the toads that hopped beside the pond, the locusts and crickets that sang day and night. But mostly, she'd love the serenity that shrouded this place. Pity, he thought, that she'd never see it.

He noticed a rotting tree across the way, damaged, he presumed, in a recent thunderstorm. He'd cut it down today and, by nightfall, he'd have half a cord of wood stacked, aging, and ready to warm him from next winter's chill.

It had taken most of the day to accomplish the task and when he was through, Cabot's bones and muscles were tense with the satisfying ache that hard work brings. He allowed himself a moment to admire the neat woodpile, then lifted the big chainsaw and returned it to the tiny shed behind the cabin. He hadn't eaten since breakfast, and his stomach grumbled angrily. Cabot could almost taste the chicken, left over from the bird he'd roasted yesterday.

An eagle soared overhead, shrieking its triumph at having snared a rabbit for its supper. It swooped low enough that Cabot had a clear view of its bright eyes. "We've both had a productive day," it seemed to say as it disappeared into the dusky sky.

After a refreshing shower, he dined by the light of a single lamp that sat on the kitchen table, then rinsed his plate and fork, and flopped into the black leather recliner that still bore the indentations of his father's muscular frame. He clicked on the lamp beside the chair and picked up yesterday's copy of *The Baltimore Sun*. Old news, he decided, turning to the "Style" section, was better than no news. Tomorrow, there would no doubt be a report about the shooting. Perhaps it would detail everything that had happened, right from the beginning. Tomorrow, he wouldn't read the paper.

He had no idea how long he'd been asleep and blamed the crick in his neck for waking him. The newspaper had slipped from his lap and lay in a sloppy heap at his feet. Cabot stacked it neatly and put it near the woodstove. In the morning, he'd use it to stoke the fire. Right now, he yearned for the comfort of his bed.

He hadn't had the dream last night and, as he climbed between the cool white sheets, he hoped it wouldn't return tonight, either. He had plenty of reminders that his life had ended the moment he had backed out of her driveway. He certainly didn't need the nightmare to confirm it. Punching his pillow, Cabot said the words he'd been saying every night of his life. "Keep it plain and simple; just talk to the Lord as though He's your friend," his mother had taught him, because that's exactly what He is."

"Lord, thank You for this day. I'll talk to You tomorrow . . . ."

He'd been saying it so long, it had become a habit. Cabot sat up in bed and tossed the covers aside, realizing he'd never really abandoned his faith. Smiling, he got up and paced around the room. He'd strayed from the straight and narrow, maybe, but he'd never actually fallen off the path. The knowledge filled him with a sense of peace and joy, and he laughed out loud.

"Lord," he said into the darkness, grinning from ear to ear, "I'm back!" He would make it. He knew that now.

☙

Elice promised herself as he drove away that she'd give him a week. If he hadn't returned by then, she'd bring him back—by the hair of his head, if necessary.

It had taken nearly three days to get hold of the police officer who'd taken the information from Cabot. In the ten days since she'd last seen him, Elice had made a few decisions.

First, she'd make him see, once and for all, that he hadn't been responsible for anything that had happened. If it took the rest of her life, she'd convince him of that.

Second, she'd force him to admit that his belief in God had never faltered, not really. She'd point out all his wonderful qualities, and prove to him that it had been his faith that had made him such a decent, caring man.

Third, she'd get him to agree to a June wedding. Elice had always wanted to be a June bride.

The Glassers had taken the kids to Williamsburg for the weekend. They'd loaned her their second vehicle, a blue, long-bed pickup that Bob Glasser used to haul wood and groceries and supplies for his dollhouse-building hobby. It took a while to grow accustomed to maneuvering the big truck but, after an hour on Route 70, she'd started to enjoy the high driver's perch and the power of the engine so much that she decided to trade in the Vega for one just like it.

The officer had been very helpful, drawing her a detailed map. He could get her as far as Route 68, he told her; after that, she was on her own. So Elice stopped at the Hancock Park 'n' Dine, ate a hearty meal, and asked the restaurant patrons who shared the lunch counter with her if they had any idea where Artemas, Pennsylvania might be. Advice came from all sides. Everybody up there, it seemed, knew George Murray. And everybody had a different way to find his mountain cabin.

Elice sat in the truck cab for a good fifteen minutes, sifting through the stack of paper napkins, each of which bore contrasting routes and different maps drawn with the waitress' blue ballpoint pen. The common denominator, she decided, was the intersection of Old Cumberland and Mount Hope Roads. If she made it that far, the old man in the coveralls had told her, she'd be able to see the peak of the Murray cabin roof. She took a deep breath and pointed the truck north. "Be my navigator, Lord," she prayed as she shifted into first gear.

❧

Cabot stood back and surveyed his well-stocked pantry. He could easily tough out a long, hard winter up here now. Never mind that it had taken two-hundred-fifty dollars and fifteen bags of groceries. And never mind that he'd cleared nearly every shelf at Helmick's Corner Store in nearby Flintstone, Maryland to do it. His goal in stuffing the Jeep with all that food was to drive down the mountain into town as seldom as possible. He'd never been much of a milk drinker, but when the mood did strike, he'd mix up a batch of the powdered stuff. Poured over ice, a man could almost make himself believe it was really milk. He'd jammed the freezer with beef and poultry parts. The ready supply of goodies made the place feel a little more like home.

He'd just closed the door on his supplies when he heard the unmistakable sound of tires, crunching over gravel. So few people drove this far up the mountain that he was always inspired to run to the window each time he heard it, just to ensure himself the driver wouldn't be pulling into the narrow, uphill drive that led to his hideaway. This time, in place of the relief that washed over him as a vehicle shot on by, a sense of doom invaded him, for a shiny blue pickup headed his way.

For an instant, he considered drawing all the blinds, turning down the radio, pretending no one was home. But the smoke, billowing from the stovepipe, was a dead giveaway that someone, recently, had been here. He'd just have to hope that this unwanted, uninvited visitor was lost. He'd give the misguided fellow directions and send him on his way.

He turned down the flame beneath the coffeepot and stepped out onto the porch, waiting for the driver to exit the pickup and tramp across the grass toward the cabin's only entrance. "Well, what do you know," he said to himself, instantly recognizing the dark curls that surrounded her lovely face.

She waved and smiled, and ran toward him. Cabot thought

of that ancient butter commercial, where the lady and the man ran in slow motion across a sunlit field of wildflowers, arms outstretched, grinning like hyenas, until they met at last, and he lifted her off her dainty feet and twirled her, causing her dress to float on the breeze. He didn't know how it had happened, but suddenly Cabot found his arms full of her. She felt good, too good. He hadn't realized how much he'd missed her.

He looked into her face, unable to hide his joy. "What are you doing up here? How on earth did you ever find this place?"

She smiled. "Heavenly navigation," she explained.

The smile faded somewhat. "Are you okay?" she asked, taking a step back. "You look terrific, I'll say that much for you."

And he did, too. It hadn't even been two weeks since she'd seen him last. But the dark circles under his eyes and the lines around his mouth had disappeared. He was wearing faded, work-worn jeans and that denim shirt she liked so well, its sleeves rolled up past his elbows, revealing his muscled, tanned forearms.

"You didn't answer my question," he said. "What are you doing here?"

She glanced at the cabin. "Aren't you going to show me around?"

He followed her gaze, then shrugged. "There's not much to see."

Elice frowned. "You don't seem very happy to see me. Maybe I should have called first."

Cabot grinned at that. "Wouldn't have done much good. I don't have a phone up here."

She nodded, her frown intensifying. "I'm not surprised. What would a hermit want with a communications device?"

He ignored her sarcastic remark. "There's a pot of coffee on the stove. Can I interest you in a cup?"

Again she glanced at the cabin. In her moment of hesitation, she seemed to be debating whether or not to stay; seemed to be trying to determine whether or not she was welcome. Without a word, she headed for the porch.

Her tiny gasp echoed throughout the cabin's interior when she stepped inside and visually inventoried the paneled walls, the braided rugs, the comfy, overstuffed furnishings, and the wide, uncovered windows. "Oh, Cabot," she said, "what a wonderful place!"

He filled two mugs with hot coffee and put them on the kitchen table. "Have a seat," he said, pulling out an old wooden chair.

But she ignored him, and wandered around, mesmerized by the place. "It's like a little bit of heaven," she said, looking out the big window. "What I wouldn't give for a view like that!" After a long moment, she turned from the scene and began inspecting the inside of the cabin, opening and closing doors and drawers, peeking into every nook and cranny. When she saw the huge food supply, she faced him. "How long do you plan to stay up here?"

"Permanently." He sat at the table.

She didn't even try to hide the disappointment his answer inspired. Elice sat across from him. "Well, I can hardly blame you. It's positively beautiful here."

He leaned back in the chair. "You still haven't answered my question."

The silence, thicker than the trees in the woods across the way, separated them. She broke it when she said, her voice a near whisper, "It's time for you to come home, Cabot."

"I am home."

The bluntness of his response rocked her. He knew because her beautiful brown eyes widened momentarily, then focused on her hands, which she'd folded primly on the table top.

She took a deep breath. "I called the detention center before I left," she said. "The duty officer said Jack's shoulder is healing nicely. He was in the hospital for three days, you know, with a policeman posted outside his door, before they carted him off to jail."

Cabot shrugged. Did she expect him to be relieved? Was she waiting for him to say he regretted shooting the maniac? He'd done what he'd had to do, plain and simple. She'd have to wait a long time before he'd admit anything else.

"His trial is scheduled for next week. The officer who gave me directions to this place told me Jack probably wouldn't get more than a couple of years. His attorney entered an insanity plea."

He grunted. "Now there's a news flash for you."

Elice's brows came together above her dark eyes. Then, as though he hadn't spoken, she said, "I don't think I'll ever forget that scene. All that blood. You could have killed him."

Cabot winced. How many times was she going to beat the fact into him?

"But you didn't. You only did what you had to do to keep him from hurting Walter."

He stared into her eyes. He'd been trying to convince himself of that ever since he had got here. Could it be she didn't view him as the bad guy, after all?

"I was just about to make myself a sandwich." Standing, he added, "Can I make you one for the road?"

"Aren't you the master of subtlety!" she said.

He ignored her sarcasm.

Elice was on her feet in an instant. "I'm not leaving here without you. You may as well get that through your thick skull, Cabot Murray."

Facing her, his brows rose and he grinned in spite of himself. "How do you propose to get me out of here? Toss me over your shoulder? Drag me by my heels?"

"I'm prepared to do whatever it takes."

He could see by the set of her jaw that she meant it. At least, she meant to try.

And then she began outlining the decisions that had inspired this trip. "Number one," she said, holding up one forefinger, "you will admit you are not responsible for anything bad that happened in Freeland." Another finger popped up. "Number two, you are a God-fearing Christian, with a mountain of faith living in your heart. If you weren't, I could never have fallen so helplessly head over heels in love with you." The finger that still wore his diamond joined the other two. "And you will meet me at the altar on June tenth, because I'm changing my last name to Murray on that date, and I'd look pretty silly standing up there without you."

He couldn't move. Couldn't speak.

"So here's the deal," she continued. "We'll have a light lunch, and then you'll show me around the place. I think it's a good idea for me to know my way around, since we'll likely be spending a lot of weekends up here once we're married. And then I'm going to follow you down that mountain road, back to Freeland. Back home, Cabot," she said, shaking her finger under his nose, "where you belong."

He grabbed her finger, and his hazel eyes drilled into her dark ones. "Ever since I got here, I've been praying for a sign of some sort. Something that would tell me whether or not I'd done the right thing by leaving." His arms went around her. "How does it feel to be a messenger of the Lord?"

A Letter To Our Readers

Dear Reader:

In order that we might better contribute to your reading enjoyment, we would appreciate your taking a few minutes to respond to the following questions. When completed, please return to the following:

Rebecca Germany, Editor
Heartsong Presents
P.O. Box 719
Uhrichsville, Ohio 44683

1. Did you enjoy reading *Pocketful of Love*?
   ❏ Very much. I would like to see more books
      by this author!
   ❏ Moderately
      I would have enjoyed it more if _____

   _____

2. Are you a member of *Heartsong Presents*? Yes   No
   If no, where did you purchase this book? _____

   _____

3. What influenced your decision to purchase
   this book? (Check those that apply.)

   ❏ Cover   ❏ Back cover copy

   ❏ Title   ❏ Friends

   ❏ Publicity   ❏ Other _____

4. On a scale from 1 (poor) to 10 (superior), please rate the following elements.

    ___Heroine   ___Plot

    ___Hero   ___Inspirational theme

    ___Setting   ___Secondary characters

5. What settings would you like to see covered in *Heartsong Presents* books?

6. What are some inspirational themes you would like to see treated in future books?_____

7. Would you be interested in reading other *Heartsong Presents* titles?   ❑ Yes   ❑ No

8. Please circle your age range:
❑ Under 18   ❑ 18-24   ❑ 25-34
❑ 35-45   ❑ 46-55   ❑ Over 55

9. How many hours per week do you read? _____

Name _____

Occupation _____

Address _____

City _____ State _____ Zip _____

Veda Boyd Jones

___*Gentle Persuasion*—Dallas Stone, former major league pitcher, represents everything Julie Russell despises, yet she is strangely drawn to him. Can gentle persuasion help both Julie and Dallas find room for each other's gifts? HP21 $2.95

___*Under a Texas Sky*—Abby Kane is caught in a stampede of emotions when her hometown is selected as the location for an upcoming movie. Called in to assist screenwriter Rob Vincent, Abby is soon captivated by both the process of making movies and the man himself. HP34 $2.95

___*The Governor's Daughter*—Landon shares Gayle's faith in God and her fascination with politics, but Gayle resists his attempts to discover her true identity. Hurt once already, she has no desire to be loved only as the governor's daughter. HP46 $2.95

___*A Sign of Love*—Andrea Cooper is comfortable with her life as a high school history teacher, president of the local historical preservation society, and active church member. Comfortable, that is, until Grant Logan bursts into her life. HP78 $2.95

....Heartsong ♥ng ....

..... Presents ....

Great Inspirational Romance at a Great Price!

Heartsong Presents books are inspirational romances in contempo-
rary and historical settings, designed to give you an enjoyable, spirit-
lifting reading experience. You can choose from 88 wonderfully writ-
ten titles from some of today's best authors like Colleen L. Reece,
Brenda Bancroft, Janelle Jamison, and many others.

When ordering quantities less than twelve, above titles are $2.95 each.

SEND TO: Heartsong Presents Reader's Service
                P.O. Box 719, Uhrichsville, Ohio 44683

Please send me the items checked above. I am enclosing $
(please add $1.00 to cover postage per order. OH add 6.5% tax. PA and
NJ add 6%.). Send check or money order, no cash or C.O.D.s, please.
          To place a credit card order, call 1-800-847-8270.

NAME _____

ADDRESS _____

CITY/STATE_____ ZIP _____

LOVE A GREAT LOVE STORY?

Introducing Heartsong Presents —
Your Inspirational Book Club

Heartsong Presents Christian romance reader's service will provide you with four never before published romance titles every month! In fact, your books will be mailed to you at the same time advance copies are sent to book reviewers. You'll preview each of these new and unabridged books before they are released to the general public.

These books are filled with the kind of stories you have been longing for—stories of courtship, chivalry, honor, and virtue. Strong characters and riveting plot lines will make you want to read on and on. Romance is not dead, and each of these romantic tales will remind you that Christian faith is still the vital ingredient in an intimate relationship filled with true love and honest devotion.

Sign up today to receive your first set. Send no money now. We'll bill you only $9.97 post-paid with your shipment. Then every month you'll automatically receive the latest four "hot off the press" titles for the same low post-paid price of $9.97. That's a savings of 50% off the $4.95 cover price. When you consider the exaggerated shipping charges of other book clubs, your savings are even greater!

THERE IS NO RISK—you may cancel at any time without obligation. And if you aren't completely satisfied with any selection, return it for an immediate refund.

TO JOIN, just complete the coupon below, mail it today, and get ready for hours of wholesome entertainment.

Now you can curl up, relax, and enjoy some great reading full of the warmhearted spirit of romance.